THE LOST NAME SOCIETY

For Hish and Jad,

And for my mum Krishna and my late dad Kewal Krishan.

The Lost Name Society is a Fox & Ink Books book

First published in Great Britain in 2026 by
Fox & Ink Books
Part of the University of Lancashire
Preston, PR1 2HE, UK

978-1-917894-24-1

1 3 5 7 9 10 8 6 4 2

Set in 10/16pt Kingfisher by Amy Cooper.

A CIP catalogue record for this book is available from the British Library.
Printed and bound in Great Britain by Clays Ltd, Elcograf S.p.A.

THE LOST NAME SOCIETY

S R Krish

Fox & Ink Books

Chapter 1

The wrought iron gates swing open and the bus chugs up the long driveway towards the school. I swivel in my seat to see the gates clang shut, sealing me in. We're in the middle of absolutely nowhere, with only trees for company and a sleepy village way down the road. That's bad enough, but the high gates and steel fencing enclosing the school grounds feel like overkill.

I turn back around and take a breath. I'm here for induction week. All the students on this shuttle bus are in the same boat as me, but it doesn't feel that reassuring, nor does sharing a dorm with strangers. No one's talking much – probably apprehensive, like me. But I'm hopeful too. This place has a good rep.

I've finally arrived at Merrybourne School, an elite boarding school in the Cotswolds. All through the summer my parents have been finding creative ways to tell me that I need to excel when I get here. As if I don't know that; as if I don't want the same thing. That's why I'm here. Year nine to year thirteen, and then on to a top uni – that's my plan. I was given that board game *Operation* when I was six years old, and the buzzer never went off for me. Not once. "With those steady hands you could be a surgeon one day, Andy," Dad had said, laughing (he always lost when we played), and that kind of planted the seed in my head.

As the school building comes into view, a shiver runs down my spine. The weak autumn sun is obscured by brooding clouds, casting shadows across the grounds and shrouding the buildings ahead in darkness. I take in the five towers, the ugly stone faces and strange creatures sitting guard on the roof, the huge arches, the jagged pinnacles and spires reaching up and disappearing among the black clouds. Eat your heart out, Count Dracula.

The bus driver opens the doors, and we gather our stuff and file up to exit the bus.

"Good luck to you," the driver rasps as I'm about to step off. I turn back to say thank you but he's giving me this weird look through his rheumy eyes, so red it's a wonder he can see to drive. His gold tooth catches the light, glinting menacingly. I jump down, half afraid that he's going to lock me in the bus with him, and hear him cackling to himself as the doors *whoosh* shut and he drives away.

Our feet crunch across the gravel driveway as we head towards the massive wooden doors in the arch where some students are waiting to show us around. I have no idea where my dorm is, but hopefully it's cosier than this building with that pair of monstrous gargoyles leering at me from their perch above the doorway. Their bulbous eyes seem to track me.

"Hey."

Someone taps me on the shoulder and I almost jump out of my skin. I turn around to see a girl grinning at me, her hands raised apologetically. She's dressed in the Merrybourne uniform: black blazer with a gold and maroon striped tie, white shirt and a grey skirt. But she's projecting her individuality with blue eyeshadow, black lipstick and Doc Martens, her thick afro hair a cloud around her face.

"Sorry, I didn't mean to scare you," she says. "You looked lost, so I was going to ask if you need help finding your way around."

I flash a smile, embarrassed. "It wasn't you – it was those freaky little monsters." I point at the gargoyles.

"Don't worry about them. They're not gonna jump down and bite you!" She laughs.

I feel foolish now. "I'm Andy, Andy Chopra."

"Cool . . . I'm Murk, Murk Campbell," she says, mimicking my formal greeting with a grin.

"Cool," I mimic back with a laugh.

"I'm one of the 'student liaisons'," her fingers make air quotes, "sent to put you newbies out of your misery. And to show you around, of course."

"Cheers, Murk."

"It's a bit of a maze, but within a week you'll know your way around, trust me," she says. "I'm in Statue House. Have you been told which one you're in?"

"Charter House."

"OK, that's on the other side of the central area: the Pentangle – we just call it the Tangle. Follow me." She leads the way through the imposing building with its wood-panelled corridors and high-arched ceilings. We pass other wide-eyed newbies being guided by student liaisons. "Over there is the main hall for assembly, and out here," she says, stepping through a wide door, "is the Tangle.

You pretty much have to pass through it most days to get to lessons and to your house."

We had a sad concrete square at my old school. Here, the middle of the Tangle has a bubbling fountain as its centre-piece – OK, it's got these hideous creatures spitting water, but still. It's banded by trimmed hedges and a manicured lawn, not a blade of grass out of place. Cutting through the lawn are stone-flagged paths.

"Those paths lead to the five houses. The school is laid out like a pentangle with one of the five houses and their tower on each point, and the Tangle at the centre. You won't get too lost if you think of it like that," Murk says, pointing to the five points beyond the Tangle. "Charter, Oak, Well, Statue and Adder."

"Like the snake?" I ask.

"Yeah! Don't worry, though – the only snakes here are some of the students." She winks.

"Oh. Now I *am* worried."

"I'm sure you'll fit in fine, Andy. Me, I'm into comics, gaming and doing my own thing. And that seems to be a problem for some of the kids here," she says, with an eye roll.

"Isn't everyone into comics?" I say.

"Know what, Andy, I think we might get along real fine! So, back to the boring stuff I'm supposed to be telling you. The school's got shed loads of history and five tenets. It's all a load of *blah, blah, blah.* Students are pretty diverse 'cos it's a state-run school. But if you venture down to that pretty little village, it's *qwhite* a different matter, if you get me. Although, they seem to dislike all Merrybourne students equally, whether you're white, or black or brown. So, watch out," she says, wagging her finger.

"Really? I didn't see much of the village when I was waiting for the shuttle bus at the train station. Looked twee, you know, like a postcard."

"Appearances can be deceptive," Murk says. "So, where's home?"

"A boring old no-mark town in Kent. I stopped in Oxford for the night and got the train to Merrybourne this morning."

"Oxford? Ah, to visit the uni," she says, penny dropping.

I shrug. "Parents thought it would be a good idea." I did too, but in my last school no one liked a swot, so now I keep my ambitions to myself.

"Let me guess, you want to be a lawyer or a doctor or a banker or a politician?" She ticks them off on her fingers. "Hey, I'm not judging you. This is Merrybourne after all," she says, noticing my frown.

"Surgeon, maybe," I admit.

"Good for you. Wish I knew what I wanted in year nine. I'm in year ten now and still clueless. What was Oxford like?"

"It was OK."

Mum had read the uni prospectus, 'Grand old buildings built of honey-coloured stone nestled in rolling hills', and it was exactly like that. Just like Merrybourne village too. Picturesque. And nothing like *this* place, I realise, as Murk shows me around the school. Some old places have a good vibe. Jury's out on Merrybourne School, and if it weren't for Murk's company, I'd be feeling well creeped out in this dark gothic relic.

"How many new boarders this year?" I ask, changing the subject.

Murk shrugs. "About seventy-five of you and then twenty-five of us seniors to help you settle in. Feels a bit soulless at the mo but once school starts and the rest of the students are here, it'll get better. Make sure you go home for the holidays – you don't want to be stuck here when it's empty.

"OK, here we are: Charter House. There should be a welcome pack for you in there with maps and other bumf. You go and get unpacked and I'll catch you later, Andy." She saunters off. Shame she's not in my house, she seems fun. Hope I do catch her later.

I head into the entry hall and the wall lights flicker as if in greeting. I listen. All I hear is silence, and I'm tempted to step back outside and wait for the other students to arrive, but that would be admitting defeat. On the sideboard the welcome packs are laid out. I snag the one with my name on it and take the stairs to the dorms. I dump my stuff on a bed in one of the dorms, picking one next to the window. Outside, the sky is still littered with dark, heavy clouds brooding over the school. Something flies past the window and I jerk back, before peering out to see a bat. Whoa! I thought they only came out at night.

Now that I'm on my own, without Murk's easy smile and banter, and only the odd bat for company, I feel a sudden pang of homesickness. I grab my phone. My little brother Vikram wanted a video of the school, and it's time my parents got a good look at where they sent me. I press record on the camera app.

"Hi Mum, Dad, Vik! I'm here! So, this my house. There

are six of us to a dorm and I'm the first to arrive," I say, beginning my commentary. "That's my bed by the window. Out here is the first-floor landing, and that's the staircase down to the hallway." I pan the camera around before heading down to the hallway.

"Charter House is your basic gothic house, with wood-panelled walls, dim lighting, stained-glass windows, and they've even chucked in the full creepy feel for free – I saw a bat, I kid you not! Dad, you'd love it, but Mum, you'd definitely struggle here. Nothing is less than 300 years old, and I know you only like a new-build. And Vik – trust me, bro – I'd think twice about coming here."

I move the camera around the hall and notice a glass cabinet. Inside is a huge red leather-bound book on a stand. It must be important for it to be kept protected behind glass. The top of the open page is dated with the year 2000, so these must be the students who were here twenty-five years ago. The book has thick gold-edged pages and the open leaves are bordered with an intricate design of intertwining lines of black and green with dots of red. It's like an old parchment or manuscript. Wait a minute – they're not lines, they're snakes. Weird! I peer closer. It's full of names written in deep green ink. Beside the book is a pot of ink and a long black feather. No, not a feather – it's a quill. Who writes with a quill in this century?

I leave the building and step outside. "Now we're in Charter House quad, and maybe if the sun were shining, the school might not look like a haunted house straight out of an old horror film . . . and you might now be regretting that you sent me here—"

A girl walks into shot. Her long, dark glossy hair swishes as she turns to look directly into the camera. High cheekbones, gorgeous smile, eyes like smoky quartz. She looks Indian like me, but then she could be from anywhere, I guess. People often think I'm South American. She winks at me and I realise I'm still filming her. I hurriedly turn the camera off.

My cheeks are flaming as I stutter, "I'm so sorry. I wasn't filming you. I was making a video for my family and accidently got you in the shot. I can delete it if you want. Here." I try to hand her my phone. "You can delete it yourself."

She gently pushes the phone back towards me. "It's OK, keep it. But maybe I wouldn't have winked if I knew this was going to be prime time viewing for your mum and dad."

Her voice is soft and husky and completely suits her, and I'm making a complete idiot of myself. "I don't mind the wink at all, but yeah, they might get the wrong idea, I mean, *I* like the wink, it's cool, I mean . . ." I trail off, and she comes to my rescue.

"Let me dig you out of that hole. I'm Belle," she says.

"I'm Andy. Belle's beautiful. I mean, it's a beautiful name." I could punch myself right about now.

"It's short for Trixibelle – my parents think they're uber-cool," she says. "A bit too cool for me, so I go by Belle."

"Yeah, actually my real name is Aniruddha Chopra. But no one calls me that." I can't even go into the thousands of different ways my name has been mispronounced. I used to repeat it again and again for people so they'd get it right, but it was a total waste of breath. They weren't all that interested.

"Nothing wrong with that name; it's a strong one. Why don't you use it?"

"School, teachers, you know. They either couldn't say it properly or they couldn't remember it. No one forgets Andy."

"Haha, yes, you're totally unforgettable now, Andy!"

"I didn't mean it like that. I meant it's easy. I mean easier to say . . ."

I have loads of friends who are girls, so why am I crashing and burning around Belle? I run my hands through my shock of dark hair and wish I'd bothered to get a decent hair cut with good fades. For a start, it would have made me feel a bit more confident and a whole lot cooler than I'm feeling at the moment.

She mock-punches my arm. "I'm teasing you. Aniruddha's a good name. Forget trying to fit in. Just be yourself. I know what you're going to say 'easier said than done' and that's true, but you've got to try otherwise we'll all be Andys or Toms or Harrys. Anyway, rant over," she says, taking a breath. "I'm meeting my friends in the dining hall. Come and join us."

I fall into step beside Belle and begin to feel more comfortable. As we walk, I find out that she's in Oak House, which is gutting as I was hoping she was in Charter House with me. I'm yet to meet anyone from my house.

"OK, here we are," she says. "Grab a tray. My friends are over there."

Over lunch, I discover her friends are as smart as she is. Luckily, they don't mind hanging out with a newbie.

"Really, this is no different to any other school," Cameron, one of Belle's friends, says. "There are loads of cliques. Like that group over there are the cool kids – well, *they* think they're cool – and we're the brainiacs," he says without an ounce of modesty.

"Brainiacs?"

"That's what they call us," says Alex, another friend at the table. "There's a ruder name for us too, but I won't tell you what that is yet." She grins. "They're just jealous."

"You'll scare him if you carry on like that," Belle says. "It's not like you get stuck in a clique and can't make other friends."

"Like Ford," Alex says, raising her eyebrows at Belle.

"Who's Ford?" I ask.

"No one!" Belle says, blushing.

"Ford's only the King of the Merrybourne Court. Well, the tennis courts, anyhow. Belle has a thing for him." Alex glances over my shoulder so I turn my head.

"Which one is he?"

Alex points him out across the hall. "That's our Ford."

He's standing up miming something, obviously recounting a story for his friends. Athletic, good-looking and clearly popular judging by the way the other kids stare at him. I feel suddenly deflated.

"*Had* a thing for him," Belle says, looking like she'd rather the subject were dropped. "We were only seeing each other for a couple of months. Wish you lot would stop mentioning it. It's getting annoying."

At least their relationship is past tense, but I still feel a twinge of jealousy.

A harsh crackling resounds in the dining hall, like an old radio being tuned, and the buzz of conversation and clink of cutlery fades into silence. I glance around to see what's causing the noise and spot the speakers positioned in the corners of the room.

"ATTENTION," a voice booms over the tannoy. "All students must be seated in the Great Hall by one o'clock sharp for the Welcome Assembly. Be prepared . . ." the voice on the tannoy rises and then pauses for a moment. The hall waits in hushed silence. ". . . for the most thrilling opportunity: an opportunity to die for. Do not be late."

The dining hall erupts with chatter. 'An opportunity to die for' echoes around the room. What can that mean? It's only 12:30 p.m. and already students are leaving the hall. No one wants to miss out on it, whatever *it* is.

I turn to Belle. "What's that all about?"

"Our induction week was pretty lame last year, so don't get your hopes up. Might be a special scholarship or something really boring," Belle says, as we hastily finish our lunch and return our trays.

"Like being made Head Boy," Cameron says. "Top marks in maths usually gets that gig, and that would be me."

Belle rolls her eyes. "You'd definitely win for the biggest head."

"And the most inflated ego in the room," Alex adds.

"So, it's a win-win then." Cameron laughs.

Everyone groans. I like Belle's gang. It might be OK at this school.

"I had Mr Williams for maths last year. He's over by the door. He might know what the announcement was about," Cameron says.

All the teachers are in their long black robes. It must be

a thing in this school, I guess. Old school, old customs.

"What's going on, sir?" Cameron asks Mr Williams as we reach the door.

He towers above us. "You'll find out soon enough," he says. His jet-black hair is gelled back over his head, and his hooded eyes and thin lips give nothing away. "Good luck," he adds in a way that makes me think we're going to need a ton of it. He strides away, his black robes billowing behind him.

If he could fly, he'd be a crow. I'm not superstitious, but Mum is and I know exactly what she'd say now: "Look out, Andy. Hope he's not going to bring you bad luck."

Not only that; this is the second time someone has wished me luck today. First the rheumy-eyed bus driver and now Mr Williams. I glance back at the teacher, but he's disappeared down the gloomy corridor.

I've got a strange feeling that this is not going to be a regular school assembly. And not for the first time today, I'm totally creeped out by it all.

Chapter 2

The Great Hall is like stepping back in time. It's huge and cold, and grey stone and stained glass add to the sombreness, with a vaulted ceiling and muted light coming from elaborate wall sconces. I grab a seat next to Belle, near the front, where there are still some available. No one likes sitting at the front, even for assembly. The excited clamour of voices dies down as the lights in the hall dim, spotlighting the stage and adding to the frisson of anticipation. From the row of teachers seated on the side of the stage, a teacher, robed in black like Mr Williams, rises and says, "Stand up for the school motto." We shuffle out of our chairs to stand. '*Aut vincere aut mori*,' he intones dramatically.

Around me, voices rise as the students repeat the words after him. I pretend I know them and open and shut my mouth, goldfish style. I saw the school motto in the welcome pack, but didn't pay much attention to it. It means something about conquering and death. Cheery stuff, and completely in keeping with the school's gothic vibe.

"That's Mr Peach, the deputy head," Belle whispers. "Ain't nothing peachy about him, though. Oh, and this is our totally glamorous school head, Ms Merrybourne. She loves making an entrance."

From the wings of the stage a woman emerges, her high

heels clacking like nails on the wooden boards, her startling ice-blue eyes sweeping across the hall. Her gaze falls on everyone, and when it flits across me, I want to crawl under the chair and hide. It's piercing, as though she can see right through to the depths of my soul. It's a relief when those eyes move on to someone else and I can breathe again.

"Sit," she instructs. Dark auburn tresses frame a face that's so translucent white it looks bloodless; the scarlet lipstick is like a gash across her face. Her dress could be a snakeskin with its prominent dark zigzag pattern running down the front.

"Welcome to the new students joining us this year. You are the lucky ones. This is a very special year for the school. Every twenty-five years we hold the Pentangle Prize Championship for our boarders. This prize guarantees the winners a place on Merrybourne's Elite Stratos programme, which confers automatic entry into one of the illustrious Golden Triangle universities."

Wow! Already, I know I want this. I look around the hall, and it seems all the other students feel the same.

"We're so lucky!" Belle squeals. "This wasn't offered last year."

She'd told me earlier that her parents weren't pushy about her results at school as long as she was enjoying it. Seems Belle doesn't share her parents' laid-back philosophy.

The murmur of voices is instantly hushed when Ms Merrybourne raises her hand.

"The contest will have five rounds, which will test your all-round potential for greatness. We'll be testing your physical ability, and your verbal, quantitative, non-verbal and spatial reasoning."

I hear groans from some of the students around me. OK, so it's not going to be easy, but at least no one will die trying.

Belle nudges me. "Eyes on the prize and we'll be fine, Dr Chopra."

I shrug, playing it cool, kind of regretting I opened my big mouth not once but twice today about wanting to study medicine at Oxford. But, looking around me, everyone seems so driven. I guess opportunities like this are why parents pay thousands for elite schools. I hope Belle's right about winning the prize – I've got both eyes firmly on it.

Ms Merrybourne signals for quiet. "Know this: by virtue of attending this school, you have all been judged capable of achieving greatness. This is your chance to prove it. But I must warn you," the whole hall holds its breath, "the tests will be rigorous, treacherous and highly competitive, and each of the five rounds will come with a twist," Ms Merrybourne declares.

It's unnerving the way she lingers snakelike on the 's' in twist. She steps closer to the edge of the stage and points her finger at us, black polished nails gleaming in the light. "Who are the best five among you? How far will you go to grasp this opportunity? These are the questions you must ask yourselves. In a few moments, you will be asked to sign your name in the charter. It's your choice entirely whether to enter the contest." She indicates towards the table, on which sits a red leather-bound ledger, before she draws back into the shadows of the stage.

My eyes are drawn to the ledger. It looks like the one I saw earlier in the glass cabinet in Charter House.

The hall erupts with the clamour of voices. It's a no-brainer: a guaranteed place at one of the top unis. Who wouldn't sign up for that?

"Come on, how hard can it be?" Cameron says. "There might be a hundred of us in the hall, but four of the five winners are sitting right here. They don't call us the brainiacs for no reason," he scoffs.

He said four, which makes me chuffed he's included me as one of their gang. But do I stand a chance when there are twenty-five year tens to compete against?

As if hearing my thoughts, Belle adds, "It'll be like the school entrance exams, and they were light."

Alex looks worried. "Yeah, but it sounds like these tests are on steroids. Ms Merrybourne said they were '*treacherous*'."

"How treacherous can a bunch of verbal and non-verbal reasoning tests be?" I say. I hear a student in the row behind bemoaning the fact that he hates PE, and then someone else saying she can't swim. I'm pretty sure Belle's ex, Ford, would do well: tennis players are pretty fit, which I'm definitely not, but at least I can swim and run. And, right now, I'm ready to make a run towards that ledger to sign on the dotted line.

"If you accept the terms of the challenge then line up to sign your names. Form an orderly queue," Mr Peach calls.

Chairs are scraped back as students stand. I'm up in a shot and head towards the ledger, keen to show that I'm a winner. I'm there first. It *is* the red ledger from Charter House. It has the same border of intertwined snakes. Maybe the ledger only comes out once every twenty-five years for the students to sign up to the Pentangle Prize Championship, and then it gets locked up behind glass again. I grin to myself, thinking that it's only right that a Charter House student gets to sign it first.

I look for a pen, but there's only that antiquated quill and a pot of green ink. I dip the quill into the ink pot and remember Belle's words. *'Forget trying to fit in. Just be yourself'*. She's right, I have a strong name. I should use it. I start writing out 'Aniruddha' – a fresh start. But then the uncomfortable memories from my previous schools come flooding back to me; being singled out by staff and students alike for being 'different'. Besides, I was registered at Merrybourne as Andy, so I'd better stick with that. I blot out 'Aniruddha' and begin to write 'Andy'. I wince at the right mess I've made on the brand-new page and, as the first to sign, it's obvious it's me who's done it. I notice it's a four-leaf page, and no one's looking. Everyone's too busy speculating about what kind of tests we're going to face, so I take a chance and pull at the thread holding the pages together. I quickly remove the offending pages and slip them into my pocket to chuck away later, then I sign as Andy Chopra on the new page.

As I set the quill down, I do a double-take. The threads have come back together by themselves, and now you can't even tell there are pages missing in the ledger. How is that possible? I rub my eyes, but the threads are in place – *like magic*, my brain whispers. But that would be ridiculous. Right?

The girl behind me nudges me out of the way and signs the book. I hover, wondering what to do now. I can't see her name as she's bent low over the page, her black, silky hair falling like a curtain obscuring it. When she moves away from the ledger, her eyes dart around anxiously. I notice it too: the atmosphere in the hall has markedly changed. The initial excitement among the students has morphed into a very different mood – more subdued. Maybe signing that charter is like signing an official contract, somehow more serious. I don't remember ever signing my name to something like this before.

Kind of feels like you're signing your name away.

The girl turns to me as she passes by and whispers, "I saw what you did with those pages. Aren't you worried the teachers spotted you?"

My heart slams against my chest and I glance around nervously, wondering if anyone else saw.

She finds an empty seat and I park myself in the chair next to her.

"Ripping the pages out of that book was crazy. I mean, that charter is like a school heirloom. It's hundreds of years old," she whispers.

"I had to – I made a mistake. Everyone would have seen it. I'd have the whole school ragging on me for the rest of the year, and it's barely begun." I can tell she's wondering how stupid I must be to mess up writing my own name. Sighing, I explain, "Don't laugh, but I started to write my proper name, then changed my mind and just wrote 'Andy'. No one uses my real name."

She shakes her head at me, her short black hair swinging around her face. "Seriously?"

"I've done it now. Do you think anyone else saw?"

Her eyes scan the dimmed stage. "I think you're safe. And I won't be telling anyone. I'm Jane, by the way."

Jane is East Asian and I wonder if she's anglicised her name like me. If she has, I don't blame her. It's kind of what's expected of us.

"Thanks, Jane," I say, relieved. "When do you think the tests will start?"

"Tomorrow, I guess. I haven't even unpacked yet."

"Nor me," I say. "I suppose we'll find out soon enough." We watch in silence as the line of eager students dwindles down. "There goes the last student signing the book."

"No, there're still four waiting to sign," says Jane, jamming her thumb behind her.

The four students aren't approaching the red ledger. Instead, they walk back to their seats. Well, at least that's four less people to compete against.

The hall hushes again as Ms Merrybourne takes centre stage. "Ninety-six students have signed the ledger. Four of you have elected not to take part, as is your right. However, by not signing you have shown that you are clearly not Merrybourne material. You have forfeited your right to remain in the school and you must leave immediately."

There's a commotion as the four protest that they have every right to be in the school and not do the tests. One of them yells, "It's not fair! You gave us a choice!"

"Ravens, take them!" Ms Merrybourne orders.

Ravens?

Our eyes are drawn to the black-cloaked figures emerging

from the shadows. They glide through the hall, their faces concealed under their large hoods. As they converge on the four students, there's a collective gasp. The four students edge away from the advancing figures but there's no escape. Their bewilderment rapidly turns to fear as they're grabbed by the cloaked figures and led out of the Great Hall struggling and screaming.

I'm shocked and suddenly terrified that the hooded figures are going to come for me too. I desecrated the School Charter. Beside me, Jane grips the edge of the chair, her knuckles ghostly white.

Ms Merrybourne looms over us once more. Immediately the clamour dies away. Suddenly the students are no longer upset – instead, they gaze at the headmistress in pure adoration. I risk a glance at Jane. Like me, she looks scared and incredulous at what's going on. Ms Merrybourne raises her arms, her red lips part and she smiles benignly at us. "You are the lucky ones. Ninety-six of you have shown that you are ready and willing to take part in the games. Return to your dorms, put on your uniforms and prepare yourselves for the first game. You are going to have the time of your lives!"

The hall rises as one to follow her instructions. No one's talking, no one looks apprehensive or afraid. What the hell is going on?

"Is this for real?" I whisper.

Jane looks at me and I see the fear in her eyes. At least I'm not the only one who thinks something strange is going on. Even more weird is that no one speaks as we join the queue to leave the hall. There's not even a whispered murmur to be heard. Once outside, everyone heads towards their dorms, the sound of marching feet the only thing that's breaking the deafening silence. I keep my mouth shut too, but can't help questioning why not a single student is talking about what just happened in the hall.

Around the grounds there are many more of Ms Merrybourne's Ravens, dark cloaked figures with their faces shrouded inside their hoods. They're straight out of a horror film and they are everywhere I look. Who are they? Why are they standing there like silent watchers, like . . . guards? My heart begins to pound and my hands are clammy with sweat. I wipe them down my black jeans. I'm trying not to think about the Ravens, but I can't help it, they're stationed on every corner. There's only one reason why you have guards – to make sure nobody gets in . . . or gets out.

By the time I reach my dorm, my hands are shaking so much I can barely scroll down my phone to call my mum and dad. I hit call, but the call won't connect. I tap out a text message.

'GET ME OUT OF HERE!'

I type the words in block capitals so they know I'm deadly-for-real serious. I press 'SEND', but nothing happens. I stab the 'SEND' button over and over again.

I've got no bars on my phone! I head over to the window and try again. Nothing. I practically hang out of it, hoping the bat doesn't make another unwelcome appearance, and try again and again. Nothing.

There's no signal. That's odd. There was earlier. I head

down to the common room and try again. No messages are going through. I try everything. I power down my phone and restart it. Still, the message won't send. I logged onto the school Wi-Fi as soon as I first arrived, so I try sending a WhatsApp message instead. I know my parents and I know they'll come flying to the rescue if I tell them what's going on. Wouldn't they? What if they don't believe me? What if it sounds like I'm homesick and that's why I made up this fantastical story?

There's a little clock next to my message. It won't send because there's no Wi-Fi.

No reception and no Wi-Fi!

I sink down the wall, my head in my hands. There's no way of reaching them. No way of reaching anyone. And with those menacing Ravens posted in the school grounds, outside the houses, everywhere, there's no way out.

Chapter 3

The Charter House common room is cavernous and smells of musty leather and wood polish. I couldn't face dinner this evening so I came here to be alone with my thoughts. But I'm no longer on my own. Other kids have finally arrived – heads down staring at their phones, frantically tapping out messages to family or friends – but judging by their frustrated faces, no one's got any phone reception. At least they're finally talking and reacting to what's going on. The silence since everyone left the assembly hall earlier had been eerie. The only time it was quiet like that in my old school was when all the students were in lessons.

"Is anyone on the Wi-Fi? I've got nothing," one kid says.

There's a chorus of uneasy replies stating the same.

"There has to be reception somewhere. I rang my dad when we first arrived and it was working fine then," says another kid.

"Yeah, I made a TikTok."

"And I posted to my Insta stories."

Pretty soon, bewilderment turns to anxiety, and anxiety makes us overthink – including me. What if the school is stopping us from calling for help? Everyone in the room is afraid and judging by the voices speaking frantically over each other, fear is infectious.

"What a right bunch of babies. Your nanny didn't change

your nappies?" A kid speaks with that condescending southern counties RP accent. "Don't worry, you can ring Mummy and Daddy soon. It's a simple technical glitch." He's tall and stocky – probably a rugby kid. He has a buzzcut up the sides with a small floppy section of hair on top like the clippers ran out of battery before they got there. Three boys standing around him have versions of the same haircut and matching bullish expressions. They clearly rule the house with their posh accents and their don't-dare-argue-with-us attitude. It might be clever to steer clear of this guy and his crew when the games start. "Surprised you numpties even got through the entrance exams." He smirks, looking around the room, daring anyone to speak. The room goes quiet for a while. Gradually people start speaking again, but in hushed voices.

"Anyone know when the games are starting?" I ask, too loudly. I wince as Buzzcut's eyes flash towards me, and try not to look like I'm cringing away.

"Why? You planning your last rites and eulogy, matey?" Buzzcut says. His minions laugh as if it's the funniest thing ever. They huddle up, congratulating each other on scaring the new kids.

I shake my head and duck away, finding a space for myself in a corner, and park myself on the polished floorboards. The last thing I need is his attention on me.

A slight, fair-haired boy hunkers down next to me. "You OK? I think he's a year ten. Best to ignore him," he says.

"Yeah, I'm good. I'm Andy. You're a year nine too?"

"Yep. I'm Will. First time boarding and already I don't

like it here. What's with those guards everywhere? Can't believe they dragged those kids out of the hall like that."

Another kid joins us on the floor. "Hey, I'm Marco. I'm new too." He runs his hands through his thick curly hair. "Wish I'd gone with them. This school is giving me the creeps. On top of it, we've got that ogre over there thinking he owns the place, and the guards posted everywhere are right out of Mordor."

"Well, that's an interesting analogy," a girl with a blonde pony-tail says, joining our group. "You can battle ogres and orcs, but these guards are faceless, silent sentries. The way they so easily lifted those kids and dragged them out was unreal. Which is why..." She pauses, but she's got our attention. "I think it's all put on for effect. They want us scared, they want us terrified – it's part of the test, don't you see?"

"No way. I don't believe that," I say.

She shrugs. "Believe what you like. This is a test to see if we're up for the real games, and you lot are already failing." A short silence follows while we think about this theory being a possibility. "I'm Amy, by the way," she adds.

"So which game is gonna happen first, do you think? All that non-verbal reasoning stuff isn't much fun. How would it work in a game?" Will asks.

"Guess we'll find out soon enough," I say.

"Do you think they'll let us leave now? We could look for the school office and use the landline to call our parents." Will's voice is rising in panic.

We've kept our voices low, but Buzzcut still heard Will. He's over in a flash, his crew right behind him. He kicks

Will's foot and barks, "Stand up!"

Talk about a superiority complex.

Will stumbles to his feet. We follow suit – we've all met a Buzzcut type before, and there's safety in numbers. Well, sometimes. And standing up makes us feel a lot less vulnerable than sitting on the floor with this bully and his cronies looming over us with their fists balled.

"Why'd you even bother signing your name? Eh?" Buzzcut pokes Will in the chest. His crew sniggers behind him. Will's small for a thirteen-year-old, but it's what bullies always do – pick on whoever they perceive as the weakest.

"'Cos th-they asked us to," Will stammers. "We-we didn't have much of a choice."

Buzzcut mimics Will's stammer, and his cronies fall about laughing.

Maybe the girl, Amy, was right: everything is a test, and Buzzcut is just trying to get a mental edge by intimidating the rest of us. We back away. Let Buzzcut think he has the upper hand here. He'll get bored of picking on Will soon enough.

"You should've gone home with the other four losers!" His eyes flash around us, memorising our faces. "There can only be five winners. You're all going to lose, and we'll make sure of it. Won't we lads?" His team nod their heads in unison.

Will stammers something, but Buzzcut isn't listening to him. He's noticed me. "What are you looking at? Got something you want to say?" He clicks his neck to the right and to the left, like a wrestler limbering up for fight night.

I'm not going to fuel his fire by responding. I shrug and look at my feet.

"Hey, I'm talking to you, curry-head!"

Inside I'm screaming at this idiot, but I keep my mouth sealed shut. He's up in my face now with his fetid breath.

He's interrupted by a series of clicks from the speakers in the corners of the room, and then there's that crackle again before a voice over the tannoy announces: "The games are about to begin. All students must make their way to Adder House immediately."

Buzzcut and his friends cheer, and I breathe out that breath I've been holding in. Around me there's a mixture of reactions. Not everybody is cheering – some look sick to their stomachs, like Will, whose eyes dart desperately around the room searching for a way out. I know how he feels. But Amy flicks her ponytail and grins, showing no fear.

Before leaving the common room, Buzzcut glares back at me, suggesting he hasn't finished with me yet.

Out of the frying pan, into the fire.

This isn't how I envisaged my first day here would be. I was anxious, to be honest, away from home for the first time and all that, and excited too about the kids I'd meet and the friends I might make. But I never expected to feel scared the way I feel now. I'd do anything to be back in my bedroom in my little terraced house at the end of a normal suburban street where I know the neighbours, and my mates live down the road. I could be over at Hari's playing FIFA with the gang instead of here.

It's practically dark as we leave Charter House and make our way to Adder House. We join other groups of students heading the same way. Ninety-six of us are going to play a game without a clue what it is we have to do, but Ms Merrybourne's word *'treacherous'* is at the very front of my mind. It'll be doubly treacherous for me with Buzzcut breathing his stinking breath down my neck throughout it.

"Hey, Andy." Murk bounces up and walks beside me. I grin back at her. It's beyond good to see Murk with her mega-watt smile. "Saw you looking all lost and glum. It won't be that bad."

"Wanna bet? I had a run-in with this posh meathead in my house – says he's going to make sure I lose. Somehow I don't think this game is going to be much of a laugh."

"I only need one guess to know you're talking about Piers Balfour," Murk says. "Yeah, even Mummy and Daddy's influence couldn't keep him from getting expelled from some private school. But he's damned clever, and a rugby star, so the teachers let him get away with murder. Look, it's only a stupid game, and he can't hurt you. We'll stick together."

"Thanks, Murk. No offence though, but he's got back-up, and they're vile."

"Are you saying that me and my Doc Martens won't be enough?" She lifts her foot to show off her heavy-duty black boots.

"Well, yeah."

"What I haven't told you about is the black belt in jiu jitsu I've got tucked away. The sweeping lion is one of my best moves and it can take down the biggest bully. No one messes with Murk or her mates. OK?" She holds out her hand and we fist-bump.

The odds are still stacked against us, but she's made me

laugh. The laugh soon fades as Ravens materialise on either side of us.

"Stick to the path!"; "Look lively!"; "No talking!"; "Keep up!" they yell from under their cowls.

"Gawd almighty, they seriously need to chill," Murk mutters under her breath. "Summer holiday wasn't long enough for them?"

I crack a smile, despite the bubble of fear. "Any way we can duck out and hide somewhere until this game is over?" I whisper.

"Too late. That's Adder House," she says as we grind to a halt.

The large arched entrance is just up ahead. Soaring high above it is a grim-looking gothic tower complete with flying buttresses adorned with macabre stone faces, tracery windows with stained glass panels, and the ever-present leering gargoyles. My feet want to run, as does every other part of me. I take a sideways step and I'm shoved back in line by the rough hands of one of the Ravens.

"Stay in line," he hisses.

Murk pulls me beside her and squeezes my arm. "We're going to be OK."

I wish I shared her optimism.

"Single file to ascend to the top of the tower," a guard shouts.

"All must go up. But not all will come down," another Raven adds.

Ominous words straight out of a horror flick, but he's got to be joking. No one speaks like that in real life. And what does that even mean? Why will only some students come back down?

I hear the Raven repeating the phrase in the same doom-laden voice as other students file past him. I don't care what Amy said about this not being real. It feels real enough to me.

And that bubble of fear inside me feels like it's swelled enough to burst.

Chapter 4

It's only a game. It's only a game. I repeat it in my mind as we go through the arch into Adder House and start climbing the wide flagstone steps. The walls are made of thick stone, with dimly-lit lamps in wall sconces lighting our way. The only sounds are the echoing footsteps of ninety-six students.

Upwards we trudge, feeling gloomier and more sombre with each step. There's no running away now as I'm hemmed in by students in front and behind. Luckily Murk is a reassuring presence right behind me. *It's only a stupid game*, I tell myself for the thousandth time, *and I'm good at games*. And then we're at the top. The stairs open out into a domed stone hall. Our eyes are drawn to the huge tapestry dominating the far wall.

It's the school emblem: the adder. The tapestry is framed by a border of adders, their distinctive black patterning intertwining, and at the centre is the biggest, baddest snake I've ever seen in my life. It's got to be the queen adder. It's so life-like it's almost 3D, as though it's merely resting on the tapestry, watching us filing in and relishing our fear. We are her prey and it's feeding time. A sudden breeze lifts the tapestry, causing it to ruck and ripple, and for a horrible gut-wrenching moment it looks as though the queen adder is slithering off the tapestry.

We stumble back as she writhes across the tapestry, flexing her long, sinuous body. The queen opens her red mouth wide, sharp fangs glistening white in the flickering light of the lit torches to either side of it.

Beside me, Murk mutters, "It's not real, guys."

Murk might not be fazed, but try telling that to ninety-five students trapped in a gothic tower surrounded by hooded guards. Someone screams. It sounds like Will. There's a scuffle and I think he must be trying to do a runner because I hear a guard shouting, "No one leaves until the game is played."

Just as suddenly as it lifted, the tapestry settles back in place, the queen adder motionless now, her beady eyes still watching us. Nervous laughter erupts in the room. If this is all part of the fun and games then they've spared nothing on the special effects. I take a deep breath, ignoring the voices around me as I try to find that calm centre in my mind. I've got as good a chance of winning as anyone in this room. I can't let my fear win. The headmistress is obviously trying to mess with my head. I remind myself that I always ace tests and exams. I'm not going to allow myself to panic.

The door on the left of the hall opens and we're ushered out onto the roof of the tower. The half-moon glows with a pale yellow light above us, and it's a relief to be in the open air. Fresh air is supposed to clear your mind, and I need a lot of it to dispel the disturbing scenarios that raced through my head earlier as we climbed the steps of this ancient tower to face the queen adder. Someone's got major skills with that tapestry loom to weave the snake literally larger than life, and the ghoulish Ravens should get an Oscar for their supporting performance. Ms Merrybourne would hands-down win Best Actress. Imagine the fortune the school could make running these 'experiences' for people looking for exactly this kind of terror and thrill. The sinister setting couldn't be more perfect.

Then the door behind us clangs shut with a resounding thud and a bolt slides into place, and I'm brought back to reality with a thump of my heart.

The only way out is to play the game.

"Now what?" someone says. The murmur of voices rises to a crescendo as everyone speculates what the first game might involve.

"It could be the physical test," someone else suggests. But doing what? We're high up, at the top of a tower, so abseiling off the roof seems to be the general consensus, until we notice the absence of ropes and harnesses. The floor of the tower looks like it's made of square panels of reinforced stained red glass, divided by a narrow metal grid. It's strong enough for us to walk on. Not only that, the grid is numbered. It's got to be part of the game.

"One to twenty-five," Murk observes, walking around.

"Wait, there are more squares, though," I say. "Over there – they're yellow. And green to the right."

"Red, yellow, green and blue, and each section is marked with numbers from one to twenty-five."

"It's a grid. A numbers game." And it's going to be a cinch for me as, luckily, maths is the sum root of my genius. Although you wouldn't catch me dead saying that out loud . . .

A figure appears on the turret of the tower, her black robes fluttering in the breeze, and her dress like a snake-skin sheath clinging to her. She could almost have stepped off that tapestry. Raising her arms, she calls for attention. All eyes turn to Ms Merrybourne.

"The first game will commence shortly. One by one, step up and draw a lot from the box." She points to a metal box on the opposite turret. "Then make your way to your allocated spot."

We shuffle into a line and head towards it. No surprise that Buzzcut has already elbowed his way to the front, bounded up the short flight of steps and plunged his hand into the box. I get a mental image of the lid snapping shut, trapping his arm, but instead, he withdraws it brandishing a red token.

"Twenty-three," he yells, like he's already won the prize. He descends and heads for his number in the red grid.

Picking a random number out of the box can only mean one thing – it's going to be some kind of game involving probabilities: luck and chance as well as maths, and it suddenly puts a whole different slant on the game – and the outcome. I don't like the way this is heading. Nothing is a dead cert now.

When it's my turn to draw a lot, I swish the tokens around the box with my hand, my fingers curl around one, but I let go of it. I pick another and then drop it again, undecided. They all feel the same, polished tokens with the numbers stamped on them, so you can't even feel what the number might be. Three is my lucky number, seven is a close second, and then the rest of the odd numbers are good. I need to pick an odd number.

"Get a move on!" someone shouts behind me.

"Who's holding up the line?" someone else yells.

They're keen to start the game and they don't even know what it is. My dad says positive thinking always trumps negativity, so I try to think positive thoughts. But in the end I think: *Please, please, please let me be lucky. Let it be odd, don't let it be even* as I draw out a token. It's red and it's got the number five stamped on it. That's good enough for me.

I make my way towards my spot and wait. I see Murk walking towards the blue grid. She clenches her right fist and brings it across to her heart in a motion of solidarity, telling me to stay strong. I nod back at her. No one's talking now. We're waiting for our next instruction.

Ms Merrybourne leans forwards and smiles. It's a smile entirely devoid of warmth, emotionless and bleak, and it makes me shudder. "Are you ready?"

A chorus of yeses rises up. I don't join in. My heart's in my mouth, adrenaline beginning to make its appearance. I've got to stay focused, keep my head clear to win this game.

"Some of you may already have guessed that this game will test your quantitative reasoning," Ms Merrybourne continues. I hear mutters from around me. "Use your mathematical brains to reach the right answers and get to the right spots on your colour grid. Do not leave your allocated colour grid. And remember, only the right answers guarantee the safe spots."

Safe spots? What happens if you end up with the wrong

answer and land on the wrong spot? I guess the guards swoop in and remove you like they did with the four who refused to sign the charter.

"Solve the equations to reach safety." Behind her, a screen projected from the tower flickers to life in the dark sky. The digital timer is set at three minutes.

I've got this, I've got this.

"If you do not reach a safe spot, there's a penalty." Ms Merrybourne casts her ice-blue eyes across us. I wonder how many of those ninety-six faces are squirming under her glacial gaze. I know I'm one of them.

"Lights," she calls out with a clap of her hands.

The panels of stained glass in the grids across the roof suddenly light up beneath us. There's a room down there. No, not really a room. It's more like a pit. I can't quite make out what's in there at first, but as my eyes adjust to the bright light shining through the red spot I'm standing on, I see movement in the pit. I bend down to look closely. Definitely movement. Something's down there. Something big. Or . . . or lots of things. My skin begins to prickle with goosebumps. Is that . . .? Are they . . .?

It's not cold, but the goosebumps have brought me out in a cool sweat and I'm shivering. It can't be what I think. My eyes are playing tricks on me. There's no way they would do that to us. Would they? The Raven's warning comes back to me: *All must go up. But not all will come down.*

Disbelief rapidly turns to dread. All around me the air erupts with screams and cries of terror.

Beneath the glass that we're standing on is a real, live

snake pit. Hundreds, no, thousands of adders are writhing in anticipation, slithering and reaching their heads up to us, their red forked tongues darting in and out. They're eagerly awaiting the ones who fail.

If I land on the wrong spot, that's where I'll end up: in a pit of venomous adders.

It's a game of survival.

Chapter 5

1	2	3	4	5
6	7	8	9	10
11	12	13	14	15
16	17	18	19	20
21	22	23	24	25

The lights below us blink off and our eyes are drawn to the screen. Below the three-minute timer is a numbered grid of twenty-five. Deathly silence reigns as we wait for the timer to start its countdown.

And then comes a loud boom.

The timer starts.

2:59

2:58

2:57

Three equations flash up for the first round – so three safe spots, I guess. I solve them in seconds. The first one is easy:

12 + 12 – 6

It's the first equation, so I'm betting everyone will make for the number 18 panel and not bother looking at the next two. The second equation is:

20 + 7 – 5

That means nineteen have fallen to their deaths. Nineteen kids like me didn't make it. What is wrong with her? She is actually beaming with delight. How can she smile at us like that? There's no remorse, no guilt, no compassion in her dead eyes.

A girl on the green grid cries, "I want to go home. I didn't sign up for this!"

"Me too!" another student shouts. "This isn't right!"

I want to go home too, but somehow I think that's not going to be an option for any of us. Amy thought it was all make-believe. Well, she was wrong. These games are deadly serious.

A deep, low chuckle fills the air, getting louder and louder until it turns into full-blown laughter. Ms Merrybourne is laughing as if this is some kind of joke. It's as terrifying as hearing the screams of the students as they plunged to certain death.

She wags her finger at the two students who shouted out. "Once you've signed the charter there is no going home, my little darlings. There is no turning back." Her red lips part in a sinister smile. When she speaks, it's in an odd tone.

"*Everyone wants to play the games. Everyone wants to win.*"

All around me, students stand up straight and face the headmistress. Their voices rise as one as they repeat her words. I pretend to mouth them too, to blend in with the crowd. Why's everyone suddenly gone zombie-like? They've lost friends to the viper den so they should be upset, or shouting and yelling at the very least. What kind of hold has she got over them?

And why doesn't she have that hold over me?

The door behind us is unbolted and the Ravens flood across the roof, gliding among us, hemming us in. We are led back down the long flight of stairs to the bottom of the tower. No one is crying out or trying to make a run for it. How many of the students here are like me – biding their time until we're out of Adder House to make a bid for freedom?

That's when I'll make my play. I need to find a way to slip away unnoticed, then find somewhere to hide out while I work out a plan. I wish I'd paid more attention on the drive up here on the shuttle bus. I remember that we waited at the gates for them to open and I saw the high fencing around the perimeter of the school, but it can't run the whole way around because there's woodland on the grounds. There's bound to be a way out through there.

I'll have to forget about my stuff in the dorm because I can't go back there. Piers will be waiting for me for sure. There's no way I can stay here and play another one of Ms Merrybourne's sick games. I can't even bear to think about what the next game she's devised might have in store for us. More students will die – that's a certainty. Didn't Ms Merrybourne say that only five can win? Does that mean there can only be five survivors and that the rest of us will die? My hearts lurches into my stomach.

It was deeply unpleasant knowing you, Merrybourne, but I'm getting outta here.

Once we're down on the ground again, the paths are lined with more guards. I look every which way, but there is no escape. I'll have to bide my time. There's bound to be fewer guards in the dead of night, so that's when I'll either make a run for the woods, or find a cellar, where I can stay hidden until the killing games are over.

Someone draws alongside me. I glance over to see Jane. She's pointedly not looking at me.

"Look straight ahead," she hisses under her breath. I turn my eyes back to the path. "Follow me back to Well House, to my common room. We need to talk about Merrybourne."

Chapter 6

As we cross through the school grounds, a loud static crackle alerts us to an announcement coming over the tannoy system. We grind to a halt. My palms begin to sweat and my pulse quickens. I turn to Jane; her dark eyes are wide with fear as we wait to hear what they want us to do next. Surely it can't be time for the next game. My head is still reeling from what happened on the tower roof. The instinct to survive was so strong in us that we fought, punched and kicked each other. Blood was drawn. Nineteen of us fell. It would have been twenty if Ford hadn't saved my life.

"Students are free to roam the grounds or return to their houses to rest," the anonymous voice informs us over the speakers.

"Free?" Jane snorts. "I'd like to hear their definition of free!"

"Shush," I whisper, keeping my eyes dead ahead. Jane falls silent as we trudge away from Adder House.

As my eyes travel across the school grounds, I see the guards slowly fade into the background. They're more discreet but ever present. The Ravens are still watching us. This is my chance to sneak out, explore the grounds and try to find a way out of this hellhole. It's not going to be easy, but I've got to try.

Suddenly, from all around me, a chorus of voices rises as students emerge from their stupor. They're finally talking – no longer acting like zombies. Some are shocked, others seem in denial. It's a freaky delayed reaction and then some.

"Like a switch has been flicked," Jane says.

I am beginning to worry that it is just me and Jane who aren't affected by the mass hypnosis Ms Merrybourne exerts over the rest of the students. "Like they were under some kind of spell. Ms Merrybourne's no normal headmistress, that's for sure, and this school is like no other."

"You saved my life, Andy, when no one else was even thinking of anyone but themselves."

"Someone also saved mine," I say. "He dragged me up just as I was about to fall into that pit." I shudder.

"Maybe there's more of us not trying to kill anyone who gets in our way," Jane observes. "Let's get back to my house." She takes my arm.

"Wait. I don't know when the next game is due to start, but I can't stay here, Jane. This might be my only chance to find a way out of the school grounds."

"You'll never make it. Not alone. You'll get caught and dragged off to . . . wherever they took the others who refused to play."

"You don't think they sent them home?"

Jane sniffs. "Do you seriously believe they're on the train home to their families?" Her voice drops lower. "After that game, I don't believe they're even alive."

"Then come with me!" I plead. "It's crazy what's going on here."

She shakes her head. "I can't. Not yet. Will you listen to what I have to say first? Please."

There's a desperation in her eyes. I glance around. You can't see them unless you look closely, but the Ravens are everywhere, their faces concealed under their hoods. Jane's right. I'm kidding myself if I really think I can escape. I reluctantly shrug. "OK."

She leads the way to Well House. The common room almost mirrors the one in Charter House in all its grandeur. It's packed, but we find a window seat tucked away from the rest of the students. Jane half pulls the curtain across so we're not so visible.

She sits cross-legged on the cushioned seat, her short black bob falling over her face. "There's something I have to tell you. But first promise me you won't tell anyone else." Her voice is so low I have to lean closer to hear her.

"How bad can it be?" I say with a nervous laugh.

"Shush! Keep it down."

I carry on in a hushed voice. "I mean, we've just watched people trying to kill each other to survive."

"It's bad. And we both know more will die. That was only the first game of five."

"OK, I promise," I say.

"I came to this school for a reason. Years ago, my aunty, my mum's twin sister, disappeared from here during induction week. She was a Merrybourne student too."

My mind reels. "You what? For real?"

Jane nods. "It's the truth, Andy."

"Woah," I breathe.

Jane chews her lip ferociously. "Mum didn't come to this school. She and her sister were really close, and it was hard enough that they were separated and sent to different schools. And then the family were informed that my aunty had gone. Vanished."

"How could she simply vanish? Wasn't there a search or an investigation, or something?"

"Apparently she ran away because she missed her twin sister. The police investigated, but could find no trace of her. Case closed."

"But she was a kid. They don't close a case for a kid who's disappeared."

"Well, Merrybourne police did just that. Mum thought maybe it was because we're Korean, you know? Who's going to cry about it other than our small community? And they'd be rocking the boat with a reputable English institution."

"No, Jane, no way would they act that way when it's a kid that's gone missing, any kid," I say. But even as the words leave my mouth, I don't believe them myself. "Did your mum or your grandparents try going to the press?"

Jane throws her hands up in the air. "How often have you seen the press cover missing people of colour, or seen public outrage about it?"

"No. It's rare to be fair. Unless the whole community is galvanized into action, which probably wouldn't happen for a missing person, we get overlooked."

"Yes, and that's why there was zero interest in the case. Mum was never the same again. They were really close twins. She says it's like a part of her is missing, that she would *know* if her sister was dead, and it doesn't feel like she is. Mum's always searching for her, googling her name, trawling through various sites trying to find her, thinking she's seen her and chasing random women down a street only to find she's accosting a total stranger. She has good days and a whole lot of bad days in between. She's basically been having mental health struggles since my aunty vanished."

"I'm sorry. That must be so tough. I can't even imagine, Jane."

She lets my words hang for a while, the murmur of muted, anxious conversation all around us. This is so messed up.

Jane looks out of the window. "It happened right here, in this school. We've seen for ourselves what goes on here."

"I haven't even got words for what's just happened. This is no simple induction week."

Jane rolls her eyes. "You don't say, Einstein."

"I've got a theory."

"Let's hear it then."

"The school's been hijacked by a weird cult and we're caught in the middle of the cult's sick games." It sounds stupid now that I say it aloud, but what other explanation can there be?

"That's not a bad theory. Plausible. My aunty started here exactly twenty-five years ago – in 2000."

I lean forwards. "That was when the last Pentangle Prize Championship was held!"

Jane takes a breath. "Yes. She must have signed the charter in September 2000. Just the way we signed it."

"So, are you saying that every twenty-five years a bunch of students go missing and no one bats an eye?" We've just seen what happens to some of them. The viper nest still makes me shudder.

Jane draws her knees up, hugging them. "Who knows. My aunty is the only reference I have."

I scratch my head, thinking, adding up numbers. "How many students have 'disappeared' over the years they've been running this championship? Hundreds, maybe?"

Jane's eyes darken. "And no one seems bothered by it. The police in Merrybourne aren't interested. No one cares."

"How's that possible? How many families must be out there kicking up a fuss, demanding answers about where their kids are, what's happened to them, how they could simply vanish?" I can't stop my voice from rising. Jane raises her finger to her lips to quieten me down. "Sorry," I whisper. "But it's unbelievable."

"I know," she agrees. "I guess the families get ignored. It's possible they don't even know they're not the only ones to lose their kids. I need answers. I need to know what happened to her, and the only way I can do that is by playing the games."

"Jane, we could die in the next one. You won't get your answers then. Your mum would be devastated if you went missing too. We need to get out and get help. It's the only way to find out the truth."

"I've tried doing it from the outside. Trust me, the only way I can get any answers is by playing the game." There's fierce determination in Jane's eyes.

I check my phone, but there's still no signal and no Wi-Fi. "If we can get out of the school grounds or find somewhere where we can get a signal, we can call for help," I insist.

"They'll be blocking the signal in the whole area. You won't get far before you're captured."

Her words chill me to the core. "Then it looks like our only hope is to stick together, and help each other get through the next game alive."

"You've already helped me once – I'd be in the pit of vipers if it wasn't for you. I can't thank you enough for that, Andy, and for listening and understanding."

There's a tear in the corner of her eye. I lean over and squeeze her hand to comfort her. "Don't mention it."

"Thank you," she whispers, squeezing my hand back.

"To be honest, I don't think any of us has a choice. The more of us who stick together, the greater our chances of survival. And I've got an idea of who else we can ask," I add, remembering the Adder House game.

"How will we know if we can trust them?" Jane asks.

"We'll know. One of them already saved my life – Ford. Not many players were helping anyone else out there, were they? No one even wanted to share a panel with anyone else, but you, me and Ford shared that last panel. So that's three of us at the least. We've got to find more."

Beyond the curtain the common room has suddenly fallen quiet. Jane frowns at me and raises her finger to her lips.

"My heartfelt congratulations to all my wonderful Well House students!" a woman gushes enthusiastically. "You are simply marvellous and I am so proud of each and every one of you!"

We peer around the edge of the curtain to see who it is. A teacher is standing in the middle of the room, beaming and clapping her hands joyfully. She's in her black robes like all the teachers here, but it's the ecstasy in her eyes that's unnatural. We move away from the window seat and sidle surreptitiously into the crowd of students.

"That's the housemistress, I think," Jane murmurs softly. "Just as demented as the headmistress, by the looks of it."

"Time for you to run along to your own houses if you are not from Well House," the housemistress urges. "Rest and get your beauty sleep, so you're bright and alert and ready for the games tomorrow. It will be another fun-filled day for all you lucky contestants!" Her expression exudes excitement.

"Most definitely demented," I whisper back to Jane.

"Lucky? Lucky!" one student yells.

The crowd quickly parts from around him. No one wants to be associated with him. "How can you say that? How are we going survive your death games tomorrow? How can you even smile? What's normal about any of this?" the student rages.

My question too, but there's no way I'd say that out loud. I've seen what they do to dissenters. And right on cue, Ravens materialise in the common room. They make a beeline for the unfortunate student who'd been shouting at the housemistress, and start dragging him out of the common room, kicking and screaming.

My hands clench and unclench at my sides as anger and frustration course through me. If I try and help him I'll suffer the same fate – whatever that might be. So as hard as it is, I have to stay quiet.

"I hope you've learnt a valuable lesson," the housemistress says, nodding her head serenely. "It's best not to waste your energy on ridiculous protests. Far wiser to save it for the games – when you'll need it." She grins at us, revelling in our fear.

But not everyone is afraid.

Some of the students in the room are pointing and laughing at the poor kid being held under the arms by the Ravens and forcibly removed. It's a stark contrast to the mood earlier today in the assembly hall. Was that only this afternoon? Everyone was shocked and terrified when those four poor students were taken away. *Everyone.* Now they're all taking pleasure in it.

The students' behaviour is wildly erratic. One minute they're like zombies, obedient and following instructions to the letter in abnormal silence; at other times they're revelling in someone else's pain, relishing the violence and the misery.

Piers comes to mind – his face contorted with undisguised glee when he pushed me off the safe panel.

I share a look with Jane. She can see it too. Are we the only ones who can really see what's going on? She gives me a warning look to say nothing. It's dangerous to put ourselves on anyone's radar.

She's right. One thing's for sure: we've got to pretend to follow the crowd. Do as they do, act like them no matter how bad or weird that might be, so we don't stand out – whether we like it or not.

We have to be in it to win, even if it feels like we're selling our souls.

Chapter 7

When I leave Well House the night is dark and moonless, except for a scattering of muted stars. I tore a map of the grounds from a noticeboard in the foyer, which I now clutch in my hand. I sense rather than see the guards – there could be hundreds of them or just a couple for all I know. Cutting directly across the quad would put me in plain sight, so I skirt around it, hugging tight to the shadows of the buildings. Some students are still making their way to their houses, but I'm taking the scenic route back to Charter House to get the lay of the land.

It also gives me a chance to mull over what Jane told me about her aunty. She's dead, I'm sure of it, even if her mum doesn't sense it. One of those horrific games must have claimed her life at the last Pentangle Prize. Somehow the school managed to cover it up. The games could well claim our lives too, and I'm struggling to accept that Jane refuses to even try to escape. But when she agrees, I want us to be ready with a plan, an escape route, and all the allies we can get.

According to the map, there's another way to Charter House through the school grounds, so I head along a path into the gardens. They're lit with soft pinpricks of light from solar lights. It's eerily quiet. The path here is gravelled, so I tread as lightly as I can across it. The woods are a good couple of hundred metres away from the outer edge of the manicured lawns – too far for me to get to tonight without being seen. But that's got to be the way out.

I round another corner and I'm at the back of Charter House. I don't want to go in and face the rest of the students in the dorm. Exhaustion seeps from every pore in my body, but there's no way I'll be able to sleep – not without one eye open to make sure none of the other players come to eliminate me. Everyone wants to win, to survive.

The dorm is quiet. The lights are out, but the moon shines through the open drapes. Most of the students are already asleep. Now I'm glad I was the first to arrive this morning and bag the corner bed near the window. I walk across the room and glance at Will. He's lying in bed, but his eyes are wide open, staring blankly at the ceiling.

"Will? Hey, you OK?"

His eyes roll towards me. "I just want to go home."

"Same. I'll look out for you, and when the games are all done, you and me can both go home." It's a false reassurance because I've got no idea if we'll make it out of here, but I have to say something. He looks so defeated. "Try to get some sleep."

Will turns his head away from me, so I head to my bed. I don't bother taking my clothes off and, after a moment of indecision, I decide to keep my trainers on in case there are any further surprises and I have to make a run for it. When I got on the train for Merrybourne this morning, I never imagined I'd spend the first night like this. Afraid for my life. So far I've seen multiple deaths, and a headmistress who has everyone in her evil thrall – everyone bar me and Jane, and possibly Ford.

I'm exhausted but my brain is in overdrive. If I don't get some sleep I won't be alert for tomorrow – who knows what game they'll want us to play and what kind of strength it'll require. I was lucky today – Ford had my back. If there are more kids like me and Jane and Ford, I have to find them. That's my last thought as I finally drift into a troubled sleep.

***

I wake with a start and pat myself down. I'm alive. Around me kids are waking up. Most of them are still in their day clothes like me. Will's tousled fair hair emerges from under the blankets in the bed opposite mine. It's only in the light of day that I see his bruised face. His eyes are still blank. War wounds – we've all got them from the game yesterday. It's already changed him. He couldn't keep his mouth shut when we first met, but today he doesn't say a word and looks right through me.

The atmosphere in the dorm is making me anxious, so I head to the common room. A sideboard is laid out with breakfast stuff, and I grab a couple of rolls and smother them in butter and jam, before wolfing them down and venturing outside. If it's the physical test today, I'll need the energy.

Students are milling about, their mood as sombre and oppressive as the heavy clouds above. I see some groups of students in huddles, whispering, and I wonder whether alliances are being made. Everyone's got the same idea. Teaming up with others means that if the game turns brutal, as it did at Adder House, they can eliminate the weakest faster while staying protected themselves, I guess.

An uncontrollable shudder ripples through me and I suddenly want to run. To get the hell away from this place. I'm wearing the brand-new trainers that Mum bought me before leaving. I remember her telling me that the new school grounds looked amazing and it would be much nicer running around them than our local park. This wasn't the kind of running either of us thought I'd have to do. I have to remind myself to act normal. I shove my hands in my pockets to hide how much they're shaking. I need to get out of here. I want to go home.

Home, where no one wants to kill me.

I try to stay calm, but my palms are sweating and my heart is beating way too fast. I don't get panic attacks. This is fear. I check my phone for the thousandth time. No reception. No Wi-Fi. I can't do this alone. I need friends. I go looking for Jane, but she's not around.

Someone shouts, "Hey!" and I turn hopefully. My stomach drops into the soles of my shoes when I see Piers beckoning me. He starts to saunter over, his crew in tow. Somehow I don't think he's coming over to ask me to join his gang. He'll want to pick up where he left off before the tannoy announced the first game. It's time to disappear. I don't care if the guards see me running – I'm not hanging around to find out what Piers has in store for me.

I spin around and stride down a path, and then swiftly down another, before breaking into an all-out run, making doubly sure I've lost them. I don't see the girl cutting across in front of me until I've collided into her. "Sorry," I mumble as I take off again.

"Wait. Andy? Are you OK?"

It's Belle. I could hug her. I want to hug her. She made it through the last game too, but it's taken its toll. There are black rings under her eyes. "Yeah, just about. There's a guy in my house who doesn't like my face. I think I've lost him for now. He almost took me out in that game yesterday." I notice the sadness in her eyes. "It's good to see you, Belle. I'm really glad you made it. What about your friends? Alex and Cameron?"

Belle opens her mouth to answer, but the speakers positioned on the corners of the buildings come to life with the ominous crackle that seems to precede a game. My pulse quickens in response. We wait in anxious silence for the inevitable announcement.

"Students, you will each find a Merrybourne sports kit on your beds. Get changed and make your way to Oak House immediately."

The tannoy clicks off. Around us, students are already scrambling to their dorms. There are muttered voices and a few raised cries, but they're quickly quietened as Ravens appear in the grounds and stand watch.

I glance at Belle. Her shoulders have dropped, her eyes focused on the ground. She starts walking, but she's dragging her feet. Her breathing is ragged.

"I can't do this again."

"We'll stick together for this game," I tell her. I hope, like me and Jane, she's completely free of Ms Merrybourne's control. But even if she's not, I can't just turn my back on her.

"Thanks, Andy. I'm going to need all the help I can get. I

lost two friends yesterday. Cameron's gone. I tried to help him, but . . . he ended up falling into the pit. Alex too." Her voice trembles, and when she looks up at me, tears are tracking down her face. She hastily brushes them away.

"Oh Belle, I'm so sorry." I'm fighting to keep my voice down, to not attract attention, but I'm so angry.

"It's unbelievable. What's going on? It was nothing like this last year." She sobs and I take her hand and squeeze it.

"Belle, someone really tried to kill me in the first game. Were any students you knew from your year group acting way out of character? Like, they weren't in control?"

Belle studies me closely. "Yeah. A lot of the students have been acting like they're in some kind of trance – even Cameron went strange during the game. He shoved me off a panel when we could have shared it, but it turned out it was the unsafe one." She wipes the tear tracks from her face, and now I know for sure that she's free from Ms Merrybourne too. "You've got to be careful. Don't let on that you're still one of the normal ones."

"Who's normal?"

Belle and I turn towards the speaker with a start. I'm relieved when I see it's Jane.

"The three of us, for a start," I answer. "Belle, this is Jane. We're sticking together and watching out for each other."

Belle wipes the tears from her face and strains a smile. "Good to meet you, Jane. Andy's right, we need to stick together to get through this."

Jane brushes a strand of dark hair behind her ears, regarding us with a cool stare. "Yeah, sure."

I'm baffled by her frostiness, and wonder if she's annoyed because she thinks I've told Belle about her aunt. "If we can grab Ford, that'll be four of us watching each other's backs," I plough on. "I owe my life to Ford – he pulled me up as I was falling."

"I'm glad he's one of us. We might stand a chance then," Belle says.

Jane gives Belle an appraising glance, her eyes taking in the fact that I'm still holding Belle's hand, and her mouth tightens.

I let go, self-consciously. "Belle lost her friend Cameron yesterday," I explain. "She's safe, Jane. Trust me. If we're going to stay here then we're going to need to trust each other to survive."

***

Standing in front of the grand entrance to Oak House is the gigantic burnt-out stump of an oak tree. Judging by the sheer width of its diameter it must be ancient – at least 300-400 hundred years old. We await our next instruction in pensive silence. Guards are lined up behind us. The game will begin soon – whatever it is.

Our eyes are drawn back to the base of the stump as it begins to glow red, softly at first and then getting brighter and brighter. The earth around it buckles and tears, churning as thick roots appear, pulsing and throbbing. We watch in awed silence as the tree harnesses some kind of power and slowly comes to life. What kind of freaky magic is this? What kind of place is Merrybourne?

The stump of the tree grows ever taller, reaching for the

sky as branches shoot out from the trunk, gnarled and covered in vines and leaves. The noise is immense with the wood cracking and groaning as it disgorges itself from the ground. Soon it's towering above us.

And then it shudders to a stop.

Ms Merrybourne steps out from behind the huge tree. "Welcome to Oak House. Here you will contest the second game. It's a test of your physical strength and prowess."

So, we have to climb the tree. I've climbed loads of trees in the park opposite my house, and this one doesn't look too hard at first glance. But I know there's got to be a catch to this. A very lethal catch.

"Of course, you'll encounter each other as you climb, but that's not the whole story." She smiles her cold smile. "There will be other dangers along the way and you'll have to avoid them if you have any hope of reaching the top."

We strain to peer more closely at the tree. There's movement, and for a second I think it's adders again, but no. Some of the vines are moving. And there's a buzzing, soft at first, and I see wasps, but then the buzzing gets louder and louder – way too loud to be the wasps. It's like an army of drones are descending. Hornets! The tree has hornets' nests, slithering vines, and what else?

"There may be a Venus flytrap or two hidden in the tree, and poisonous plants aplenty," Ms Merrybourne says gleefully. "Lots of hidden treasures to make it all the more fun!" She claps her hands, her head thrown back and her mouth open wide in manic laughter.

No one else is laughing. Everyone is already searching for

a route up that looks the least hazardous. We have to avoid the lethal vines, the hornets that are as big as our fists, and plants full of venom that we can't even see.

"This game will require you to use your physical strength and your brains too." Ms Merrybourne taps her head. "What are you made of? Because only the fittest and the most cunning of you seventy-seven contestants will make it to the top. Oh, and did I mention the time limit?"

Another big screen timer lights up in the sky. It's set for ten minutes this time. I suck in a breath. Not only do we have to climb to the top of the tree, we also have to battle each other, crazed hornets and a whole host of treacherous plants and do it before the timer hits zero.

What happens if you don't make it to the top in time?

As if reading my thoughts, Ms Merrybourne says, "Those of you who fail to reach the top of the tree in the allotted time will be eliminated."

'Eliminated'. The word echoes in hushed whispers around me. We know the stakes and they couldn't be higher.

I've got Jane and Belle beside me. I can't see Ford, but I wish we'd found him earlier. We could do with his strength now.

"Let the game begin!" Ms Merrybourne shouts.

A loud boom sounds.

The timer starts its countdown.

Chapter 8

For a moment, everyone is frozen to the spot. The tree is a danger zone. There should be ten-foot-high hazard signs surrounding it, topped with rolls and rolls of razor-sharp barbed wire to keep kids out in case anyone was stupid enough to think that it was cool to climb.

There is nothing cool about a tree that's erupted from the hellfire of Merrybourne.

My eyes flick from the timer to the tree. *Focus on the tree*, I tell myself. *Watch the tree, look for the dangers to find the best route.* It's not easy when all around me students have burst into frenzied action, racing for the tree, as though their lives depended on it. Which they do. They're pushing and shoving each other out of the way without a care for who they hurt in the process.

Beside me, Belle and Jane begin to move.

"Wait!" I grab their arms.

"But the timer!" Belle shouts.

"Watch first, then we move," I insist.

"What're we watching for?" Jane cries. "Because if we don't get to the top of the tree soon, we're gonna die."

"Work out the best way up," I tell them. "Or the least fatal." The tick-tock-tick-tock of the clock matches the pounding of my heart, and it's so hard to stand there and not run for the tree. My eyes are darting across the trunk, the branches, the foliage, searching for visible dangers.

I spot one: my nemesis. Piers is climbing up almost directly in front of us, two of his crew ahead of him to clear the way, and two at his back, swiping at the vines. Over on the right, I see a couple of students struggling desperately to free themselves but they're well and truly entangled in the deadly vines. Another student drops to the ground, screaming and writhing, his face red and swelling up by the second. He's followed by a girl. She's batting at her body, her face, her arms, but the wasps are swarming all over her.

I glimpse a spot towards the left of the tree where there's a gap free of students. There's no way of telling what lies further up the tree, but I can't ignore the ticking of the timer any longer. Two minutes have gone by already. "That way!" I point, and we take off, sprinting.

I hope I've picked right.

The tree trunk is gnarled and there are plenty of handholds. I grit my teeth, praying nothing dangerous is lurking in the gaps I'm shoving my hands into. I shimmy up to the first branch. Belle and Jane are seconds behind me, and together we begin climbing further up the tree.

"Stay alert!" I have to yell as the sound level has gone through the roof. Screams and shouts come at us from every direction, accompanied by the hissing of the vines as they slither around the tree. On top of that is the buzzing of the wasps, and worse, the deadlier deep thrumming of the hornets.

The students are no less lethal. Further up, two students are fighting, fists flying as they do their damnedest to knock each other off the tree. One of them goes airborne with a shriek as a vine wraps itself around him. I can't suppress a shudder. Under any other circumstances, we'd be trying to save each other, not kill each other. This is so sick.

"Ford and Murk are over there," Belle shouts. "They're in trouble!"

I spot them lower down and on a different route up the tree, but not too far from us. They're ducking and diving, trying to avoid the snapped-off branches being chucked at them from some students above. Murk loses her balance but manages to grab hold of a sapling before hauling herself back onto the main branch. And still, debris is flying down on their heads. The bullies roar with demented laughter when one of them manages a direct hit at Ford or Murk.

Murk and Ford have seen us but there's no way they can get to us while they're being pelted. It's all they can do to hold on. I have to help them, but how? I scan the tree above the bullies, and spot what I'm looking for. "Wait here," I tell Belle and Jane.

I scramble up the tree as fast as I can, glad for the hours I spent with my mates climbing trees in the park. On the branch above the bullies there's a perfectly placed solution.

I catch Ford's eye and he seems to understand what I'm about to do. He grabs Murk's arm and together they begin edging across the branch closer to the trunk. Hoping they're a safe enough distance, I kick out at the hive. It's not like any hive I've ever seen before. The hornets' nest is conical and cream coloured like a wasps' nest, but way bigger and heavier. My kick makes it swing, but it doesn't fall. A few hornets fly out and head towards me. They're huge and angry, but I swat them away. I feel sick to my stomach about what I'm doing, but there's no other way to save Ford and Murk, so I aim another kick and put everything behind it.

The hive wobbles and sways, and then it begins to fall, crashing and splitting open on the branch directly above the bullies, landing in their midst. The demented laughter turns to cries as within seconds they're swarmed by the biggest, baddest Asian hornets I've ever seen in my life. There was a nest in my local park, which had to be destroyed because these hornets can kill thirty honey bees a day. No surprise the other name for them is *Murder Hornets.* I turn away, unable to look at what I've done.

Meanwhile, Ford and Murk have managed to get across the tree to Belle and Jane and they all clamber up to join me.

Ford nods at me. "Nice one. Now we're even."

We don't hang about. A glance at the timer tells us we've only got just over four minutes left to reach the top. How did that happen? I lead the way with Murk close behind me. Ford helps Jane and Belle negotiate the trickier sections of the climb.

We're not far from the top when it happens.

Belle screams. I look down in a panic. A vine is trying to wrap itself around her and pull her off the branch. Ford is fighting it off.

"Stay close to the trunk," I yell at Murk and Jane as I speed back down past them to help Ford.

I grab hold of the vine. It's thick and sticky and slippery to touch, and its squeezing Belle's ribs so hard she can barely breath. We beat at it with our fists until finally it loosens its grip just enough for us to pull Belle free. She's blue in the face and gasping for breath.

There's less than two minutes left on the clock now.

Tick-tock, tick-tock, tick-tock.

"We have to move fast!" I shout. I pull Belle up to the next branch. Ford is right behind her. Murk is helping Jane up ahead of us – she's clutching her hand, grimacing from the strain.

"Don't touch that stuff!" Murk points at some weird looking red foliage sprouting out from around the trunk.

"Go faster!" Ford shouts. "There's less than a minute left!"

Belle's trying her best but she's struggling to breathe. The vine must have bruised her ribs. We're not far now. I can see the top of the tree. There's some kind of platform up there.

The tick-tock of the timer gets louder and louder as it approaches zero. We're dead if we're not on the platform before then. Murk and Jane have clambered up on to it. They're shouting and screaming at us to hurry.

And then the final countdown begins.

0:10

0:09

0:08

0:07

0:06

Murk is reaching down for us. I grab her hand and she hauls me up. Together we pull Belle up, and Ford follows. As we collapse in a heap on the wooden platform, panting and gasping, I spot Will. He's almost at the top, but his face is bleeding, and his hands are cut to shreds. I scramble back to the edge and reach down for him.

0:05

0:04

"Reach up!" I yell at him.

He's straining, his hand outstretched. I lie on my stomach and try to grab hold of his hand, but his fingers keep slipping from my grasp.

"Will! You can do it!" But he's shaking his head, tears streaming down his cheeks, mingling with the blood.

0:03

0:02

0:01

His face is contorted in agony. "Andy!" he screams as he slips out of reach.

0:00

He's out of time. There are other students stuck down there with him who didn't make it to the top. Their faces wear the same stricken expression.

The platform suddenly judders. We grab onto each other, wondering what the hell is about to happen now. The platform begins to move, lifting away from the tree as it glides down to the ground. We pass Will and the other students in the tree, and watch open-mouthed with horror as the vines wrap themselves around them and drop them into the pulsating roots of the tree, where they're swallowed up.

They're gone.

Once on the ground, we stumble off the platform, dazed. I could have saved Will. "I should have gone back down for him. I might have made it." I'm mumbling, in shock, upset and angry. So angry. Will didn't stand a chance. I should have looked out for him. I feel the hot prick of tears in my eyes and swipe them away. It's too late for tears.

Only Belle has noticed my distress. She rubs my arm. "You tried, Andy."

"Not hard enough. If only I'd seen him earlier."

"What happened?" Jane asks.

"Andy lost a friend," Belle replies.

"We've all lost friends," Ford says angrily.

It's true. I met Belle's friends at lunch that first day and by the evening they were dead.

"They can't be dead. It's – it's just not possible. This is all way too surreal," Murk says, shaking her head. "Feel like I'm caught in that *Soul Eater* anime. And what's with those roots? Are they feeding on the bodies?"

"Don't be stupid," Ford retorts. "You're such a nerd. This isn't one of your stupid comics."

Murk's eyes fire up, but she looks away without replying. I'm shocked by the way Ford's speaking to her.

"She's right, though," Jane says, rubbing her hand. It's splotched with livid red spots. She sees me looking at it and pulls her sleeve over it. "Some weird plant. Itches like anything." She turns to Ford. "If what's just happened isn't straight out of the *X-Files* – yeah I'm a nerd, too – then what's your theory, Ford? Stranger things are happening here than even in that *Stranger Things* series, which even you might have watched 'cos it's so mainstream."

Ford scoffs. "Yeah, right. That's me, Mr Mainstream."

Tensions are running high between us. I blame the games – no, it's Ms Merrybourne. And the death that surrounds us. This isn't the last game though, and I've a horrible feeling we're really going to need each other again. "Guys, take a breath. No use arguing when there's more of this to come," I say.

But Jane hasn't finished saying her piece to Ford. "I've seen *Soul Eater*, and there's a school and there are students, and a whole heap of monsters," she says.

"Just like here," Murk adds.

"And the other students, I mean, what's up with them? It's like they're possessed or something. They don't care who they hurt, or who they kill, to win. Murk's right. It's surreal," Belle says.

Ford shrugs. We can all see he's struggling to find a logical explanation.

All of a sudden, right in front of our eyes, the tree begins to shimmer and shake. We turn to watch as it slowly buckles and tilts, the wood splitting and grinding loudly as it collapses, folding down into the earth exactly the way it came up. And then it's nothing more than a stump again. As though it had never been the tree of death. As though nothing at all had happened here. All evidence gone.

I catch Ford shaking his head and mumbling, "What the actual hell?"

We huddle closer together as everyone looks around, eyeing each other distrustfully. I can't tell how many students fell at this hurdle. I'm sure Ms Merrybourne will enlighten us soon enough, but the ones who remain know that they need people around them they can trust to watch their backs.

We're a bit of a ragtag group, but these are the only people I trust here. "What do you think? Can we stick together through the games?"

"After what we've been through? I'd say we have to," Murk says.

Jane and Belle nod in agreement, and Ford says, "Count me in."

"And you're right, Murk. There's something bare freaky going on." I drop my voice. "The sooner we get the hell out of this nightmare, the better. We're gonna need a plan."

"It won't be so easy to disappear. We've got eyes on us all the time," Jane reminds us.

"Nothing about an escape is going to be easy," I agree. "We've got to track the guards. Work out if there's a pattern to their movements. Or a shift change or something. Until then . . ."

"We play the game," Murk finishes.

Chapter 9

Everyone goes quiet as Ms Merrybourne appears. She's beaming at us like we've just won a coveted trophy for the school instead of sending hell knows how many students to their deaths. Murk is right: this is too surreal for words.

"Congratulations to you all!" Ms Merrybourne might be smiling, but her ice-blue eyes are chilling as they sweep across us. "Fifty of you have excelled at this display of physical prowess. You've earnt a well-deserved lunch. Make your way to the dining hall. A feast awaits you!" She claps her hands and the Ravens descend upon us.

When Ms Merrybourne speaks it's as though a switch has been flicked. Everyone moves together, following her instructions; no one speaks, much less demurs. The guards channel us towards the path, and the five of us fall in, outwardly as silent and as obedient as the other students in their trance-like state.

At the entrance to the dining hall we risk glancing at each other. Murk inclines her head towards a table in the far corner, and we cautiously follow her over. As we take our seats I notice Jane's hand is livid red. I have no idea what kind of toxic plant it was she touched. There must be something we can do to help her.

"Are you OK?" I ask, looking pointedly.

Jane glances at the red blotches on her hand. "It's no beauty spot, that's for sure, and it stings like hell."

"Anyone got a first aid kit? Antihistamines?" I scan the faces at the table.

"I've got some cream – for insect bites. It's in my dorm. I'll grab it for you after lunch, Jane," Murk offers. "It might help."

"Cheers, Murk. I'll try anything."

"Is this wise?" Ford whispers. "All of us sitting together."

"Unless we can communicate telepathically, how else can we plan?" Murk replies archly.

On each table there is roast chicken, slices of roast beef and lamb, and a mountain of potatoes and vegetables and bread rolls. There's cheese and fruit and cakes, too. It is a real feast. Ordinarily, I would have got stuck in by now. A roast dinner is one of my favourite meals after my mum's dhal makhani, tandoori chicken wings and aloo gobi. But not even the thought of that or the sight of the roast makes me feel the slightest bit hungry. Fear has stolen my appetite.

Ford seems to have no problem. He piles his plate high. "Fuel up," he says through a mouthful. "Our bodies need food to recover – and to get ready for whatever the next game might be. We need to stay strong."

I know he's right. In the dining hall, the sound of cutlery clinking against plates gets louder and gradually a hum of voices adds to it. Finally, the other kids have found their voices again.

"That game was designed to kill and to maim," I say. "Just like the first one. The next three will be the same."

"I would have fallen out of that tree of horror if Murk

hadn't helped me," Jane admits. "It's lucky we have each other."

"And weird how the students have got more and more violent," I say quietly. "Like they're not fully in control of how they behave."

"But why? *We* haven't changed. We've pretty much acted in self-defence or in defence of each other. I can't say the same is true of the rest of them," Murk says.

"The games have brought the worst out in them," I add.

"And they're like total zombies when Ms Merrybourne is around," Jane says. "Seriously, not a squeak out of them. It's freaky."

Belle puts her fork down. She's only been picking at her food, despite Ford's continued encouragement to eat. "Everything changed at that first assembly. That's when things went weird. Those Ravens appeared and dragged out the four who refused to sign the charter. Then the Wi-Fi went down. There's no phone signal. We're completely cut off from calling for help."

"Everyone went mad in our common room when we realised. At least the five of us are on the same page. Because if I was on my own, I'd think I'd entered some alternate reality. Who would believe me?" I add.

"We may still have entered the twilight zone," Jane says.

"There's definitely something supernatural, or some dark forces at play here. You mentioned that first assembly when it all went downhill, Belle. Did we do something that the others didn't, or did we *not* do something that the other kids did? 'Cos I'm thinking the reason why we're not affected like the others had to have happened then," I say.

"I think you're right. We're the only unaffected ones," Jane says, spearing a potato. She pauses, looking at it. "What if we were the only ones who didn't eat or drink something that the others did? But it could be anything," she says with exasperation. She sets her fork down without eating the potato.

"It can't be in the food. That's way too random." Ford pushes his empty plate away. "And if it is, then I've just sampled everything on offer. So watch for any changes that might come over me." He pulls one side of his mouth down and shuts one eye in an attempt to look weird.

Jane slaps his arm. "This is serious!"

"Whoa. I get it. And I know it's serious. Deadly serious." Ford goes quiet. He refills his plate.

"I didn't repeat the school motto, that Latin epithet. I hadn't learnt the words," I admit.

"It can't be that," Belle says adamantly. "We've been repeating that phrase during every assembly for the past year, haven't we, guys?" Murk and Ford nod in agreement.

"It definitely didn't activate any kind of spell," Murks says. "It's got to be something else."

They all know the words to the school motto, so I figure I'd better write it down and commit it to memory just in case it comes in handy. I pull out the folded pages I tore from the charter book, and rummage around in my pocket for a pen. Of course, I don't have one.

"Anyone got a pen?" I ask.

Murk peers at the pages. "What's that?" she asks. "I recognise that paper."

Jane gasps. "Are those the pages you ripped out from the charter?"

"Yeah," I admit, sheepishly. "Hang on a minute," I say as I remember how the threads of the page had come back together. The others stare at me when I tell them about what happened. "What? What are you thinking?" It's pretty clear, but I need someone to say it out loud.

"Like magic," Murk breathes.

This time Ford doesn't shoot her his usual sarcastic look. "Gotta say that's, well, pretty gutsy ripping pages out of that charter. It's like, sacred. Not sure about why the threads joined themselves up, though."

Belle's frowning at me. "Why did you do it?"

I wince. "It's going to sound stupid, but I started writing my real name. You know, the one my parents gave me." I laugh, but it's hollow.

"Aniruddha," Belle says. "I remember."

I'm glad she remembers. "Most of the teachers and kids at my old school couldn't get their lips around it, so I got called Andy. That's the name I'm registered at this school with. So I crossed out 'Aniruddha' and wrote 'Andy Chopra'. But to anyone looking at the charter page, it would have appeared as though I didn't know how to spell my own name." I grimace. "So as I was the first to sign the charter, I ripped the pages out. Only Jane saw me do it." I turn the page over. "See."

They peer at the page. At the top 'Aniruddha' is crossed out.

Jane is first to respond. "OK, this is going to sound weird, but my real name is Ji-yeon Park. I wrote Jane in the charter."

We sit up in our chairs and lean towards each other.

That's quite a coincidence, but could it really mean anything? I wait for the others to say how they signed their names in the charter. Murk speaks first.

"OK, so *my* real name is Mercedes Campbell. But I wrote Murk, 'cos who wants to be named after a posh car?"

"And I signed my name as Belle, rather than," she clears her throat and adds, embarrassed, "my proper name – Trixibelle Clayton. Which I hate. I'm lucky it's not worse than that. They could have called me Sunflower or Moondance or something equally cringe."

Our eyes are focused on Ford now. I'm holding my breath.

Ford leans back in his chair, keeping us in suspense. "Oxford Ike is my real name. I signed it as Ford," he says. "There's aspirational, but then there's just garish! Don't need people laughing at me."

We sit back and look at each other, the penny dropping.

"None of us wrote our proper names in the charter," I say. "That's got to be it!"

"Shush! Keep your voice down. Pretend we're eating, at least," Jane says, glancing around furtively. "Last thing we want is to draw attention to ourselves."

She's so right. I reach for a bread roll and push the paper towards Jane. I break off a piece of bread and as I bring it to my lips, I say, "Write your proper name in and cross it out, like I did, because this is who we really are. We stand apart."

Jane seems hesitant at first, but the paper is passed around surreptitiously until each of them have signed it and crossed out their name.

"Now all we need is something to call ourselves," Murk

says. She twists her hair through her fingers, thinking. "How about – the Nameless?"

"Or the Last Ones," Belle suggests.

Ford grins. "We're the Invincibles!"

We all groan. None of us feel remotely invincible.

"You're so ridiculous, Ford!" Murk snipes.

"Thought you'd like that as the resident Manga-Warrior," he retorts acidly.

They're really having a go at each other, so I step in to stop it going any further. "I've got it." I write *The Lost Name Society* at the top of the page. It's apt. We've all lost our real names for one reason or another, and used a name that's more *acceptable.*

"That'll do nicely," Murk says, and Jane nods.

"Yeah," Belle agrees, chewing the end of her hair thoughtfully. "It's so wild, the fact that none of us wrote our proper name in the charter is the reason we're not affected by whatever is turning everyone else into zombies."

"So this can be *our* charter," I suggest. "Our new, united charter. Whatever we face, we face together."

"For what good it'll do us," Jane sniffs. "More people are going to be *eliminated* in the next round, and there's a good chance it could be one of us."

"That's not helpful, Jane," Belle says. "We need solutions. There's enough doubt about whether we might or might not survive the next round as it is."

"Only saying how it is," Jane snaps, then sighs heavily. "Sorry, I didn't mean it like that. I'm here to find answers too."

A look passes between me and Jane. It doesn't go unnoticed by the others.

"What's going on?" Belle asks, looking from me to Jane.

I shrug. It's not for me to tell Jane's story.

"OK, don't say anything until you hear the whole story," Jane says, and then she tells them the story of her aunty who went missing after the last Pentangle Prize Championship twenty-five years ago. "So, what do you think now?" she asks when she's finished.

"Jane told me about her aunty last night. After the first game. And after what's happened today, there's no doubt in my mind we need to get the hell out of here ASAP," I say.

Murk puts her arm around Jane's shoulder. "I'm so sorry, Jane. I can't imagine what your family's gone through. Respect to you for coming here and risking your life to find the truth."

Belle is shaking her head in disbelief. "How many have they killed! We've got to make sure this never happens again!"

"First we have to survive," Ford says. "And that's not going to be easy. What games are left to play and where?"

"Charter, Well and Statue Houses will be the scenes for Merrybourne's next three death-wish games," Murk lists.

"Non-verbal reasoning, verbal reasoning, and spatial reasoning, which don't sound like they should kill anyone." I glance at the group. "And they shouldn't – unless you're playing by Ms Merrybourne's rules. We need more info."

"The games are linked to the houses – Adder House had the snake pit, Oak House had the tree of death," Jane points out.

She's right. "OK, I can check out Charter House and see what kind of game might go down there."

"Jane, you've got Well House, and I'll check out Statue

House. It's a start," says Murk. "But don't get caught!"

Ford leans forwards. "I'll watch the guards and see if there's any kind of pattern, a break in their shifts that might help us."

"I'll do the same," Belle says. "We know the school layout pretty well, and if we stay in the shadows, we won't be easy to spot."

"Keep your heads down. Avoid eye contact with the Ravens, and don't get involved in any aggro with the other students," Ford reminds us.

Easier said than done, I think.

"Yeah, especially you, Andy," Murk says. "Piers has put a target on your back, and he never gives up."

With that uplifting thought, we file out of the dining hall to head back to our respective houses. I'm dreading going back to Charter House already.

Chapter 10

Jane falls in beside me as we head down the corridor. I know it's hard for her to trust anyone here, but I'm glad she told the others about her aunty. "We can trust them, Jane."

"I hope you're right." She drops her voice. "We've seen what Ms Merrybourne is capable of. She'll find a way to shut me up, or get rid of me and I won't get the chance to find out what's happened to my aunty. My mum . . ." Jane's voice catches. "It would destroy her."

I link arms with her and feel her draw closer to me. She's trembling and all I want to do is wrap my arms around her. "We're all here for you. And the sooner we get answers, the sooner we're out of here." I force myself to suppress the thought that running as fast and as far away as possible is the best way to survive this. I couldn't leave Jane, or any of the others, behind. Could I? I barely even know them really, but this whole experience has drawn us close together.

"Wait up," Murk calls out from behind us. "Come and get that cream for your arm, Jane. I might have some antiseptic too."

"You came prepared," Jane remarks.

"Nah, I should have brought full body armour with me, my nunchucks and my Sai." Seeing Jane's puzzled expression, she adds, "I do jiu jitsu and I've dabbled in different MMA weapons training."

"I've got no idea what a *Sai* is but it sounds dangerous." Jane turns to me. "No offence, Andy, but I think I'll be sticking close to Murk from now on."

"I'll be right beside you," I reply.

"In the right hands, they're dangerous weapons. I've only used them in the dojo where we train and only with the sensei present. Google 'em. Oh!" Murk rolls her eyes. "I mean, when we get out of here and have internet access again. Hey, and I'm really sorry about your aunty, Jane. We'll get to the bottom of why they're making us play these death games. That's a promise."

Something's been bugging me about Murk and Ford – the way he puts her down and doesn't give her theories any credence when she's basically stating the flipping obvious. And then cutting her down by calling her the Manga-Warrior had to have hurt. I go for the direct approach. "What's with you and Ford?"

There's a pained look in Murk's eyes. She presses her lips together and shrugs. "It's nothing."

Tentatively, I ask, "Did you date him too and it ended badly?"

Jane squeezes my arm in warning. "She doesn't have to tell us."

Murk erupts with laughter. "Oh, you're too funny, Andy!" she says. "It's OK. It's nothing like that." Then her smile disappears. "Sorry you had to witness that. Truth is, well, me and Ford are family. Our mums are cousins."

"For real? I'd have thought all the more reason for you two to be tight," I say.

"Ford's like the golden boy – good at everything, got smarts, got that tennis thing going for him. Gets on with everyone, likes to be liked, you get me? His whole family is like that." Murk rolls her eyes. "Me, I don't need that kind of pressure, so I don't try too hard to fit in, I guess. I thought I'd find my kind of people at school. Still working on that."

"I'd never have guessed he was your cousin. He barely even speaks to you, and when he does . . ." Jane's voice trails off.

"Yeah, it's to bite my head off. Usually he likes to keep his distance from me – I'm not cool enough for that boy." Murk's laugh is brittle. "But, hey, it's OK, 'cos I know deep down, *very* deep down, he cares." She changes the subject abruptly. "Back to the games. What's your thinking?"

"Survival," both Jane and I reply.

"OK, so let's step back from that for a minute. First we're gonna sneak around our houses to see what they might be setting up for us for the next game. It could be in any of the three houses."

"Yeah, but that might not help much. Who would have guessed that big old tree stump at Oak House was going to turn into some kind of hellfire tree?" I say.

"True," Murk agrees. She thinks for a moment. "We need to know more. You know what, we might find clues if we do some research on the three houses. It's a long shot, but we might find something."

"That's a good starting point," Jane agrees.

"OK, I'll show you where the library is – it's massive, so it might take a while to find the books we're looking for," Murk says, leading the way. "Oh, and each house has a house master or mistress and they've all got an office. We might get some intel there too, but take care – the Ravens seem to materialise out of the frickin' walls."

"And they're always watching," I add, looking over my shoulder.

"They'll be teachers, won't they?" Jane asks. "They're in on it."

"Yeah, but judging by Ms Merrybourne's freaky influence, they could be controlled by her. Remember your house mistress?"

"What was wrong with her?" Murk asks.

"It was weird, like everything here. She was so gleeful about the kids that had fallen into the vipers' nest, it was unnatural. Her face was lit up with joy. I mean, it was demented."

"And then the Ravens swooped in and grabbed that kid who said he couldn't take any more. Later, he came back because he insisted he wanted to play the games. I wonder what might've happened to him if he hadn't persuaded them to give him a chance," Jane adds quietly.

Murk gives Jane's shoulder a squeeze. "Yeah, probably best not to."

"How far's the library?" I ask. The silence of the corridors is heavy. "Guess everyone's gone back to their houses, which means we should too so we don't stick out like sore thumbs."

"It's down the end of this corridor and around the corner." Murk picks up the pace.

"I haven't seen a single guard since we left the dining hall." Jane checks over her shoulder. It's become a habit for all of us. "It's clear. Maybe they don't bother inside the buildings. They only patrol outside – to make sure no one tries to escape."

"Makes sense," I say. "There's no escape route if you're inside the buildings. Unless there are secret tunnels."

"If there were, I'm sure I'd have heard about them by now," Murk says. "But that's a good point. I'll tell Ford and Belle they could watch the Ravens from the windows inside, or duck into one of the buildings if they need to hide."

Almost on cue, we hear the unmistakable tread of heavy footsteps. They're storming down the corridor we just left by the sounds of it.

"Speak of the devils. Maybe we're not so safe from them inside either," I mutter. "We've got to hide."

"Down there," Murk hisses. "Through that door."

The thumping of boots is getting louder by the second.

"Run!" I whisper urgently.

The girls are right on my heels as we barge through the door. We cringe as it squeaks loudly. I pull it shut as quietly as I can.

We're in a disused common room judging by the pervading mustiness and the dust motes littering the air. Curtains are half pulled across the windows adding to the gloom of the room. There's sofas and chairs dotted around, and dusty tables lining the wood-panelled walls. Faded portraits of old Victorian men and landscapes of English countryside in gilt frames adorn the walls. There's a grandfather clock along one wall, its pendulum swinging. Someone must come in here to wind it up, but those footsteps didn't sound like a caretaker out there in the corridor – there were way too many of them.

Murk points. "Get behind the sofa by the window."

We wedge ourselves in behind it, trying to catch our breath. Murk raises her finger to her lips just as Jane sneezes. Her hands fly to her face, covering her nose and mouth. "The dust," she whispers, "I have allergies." She sneezes again.

"They didn't see us," I say in a hushed whisper. "I'm sure of it."

"Let's give it a few minutes," Murk says softly. "To make sure."

We wait, listening in tense silence, the only sound our soft breathing. Jane's kept her hands over the lower part of her face, and her eyes are squeezed shut, trying to keep the sneezes in.

The footsteps stop right outside the door.

I'm still sure they didn't spot us. But I could be wrong. Why would the Ravens bother following us? It's not as though we were doing anything wrong. Were we instructed to go back to our Houses straight after eating?

I don't want to be one of the ones who gets dragged away by the Ravens. The ones who failed in the tree were sent down with the roots of the hellfire oak. Is that where they take us? I can't get the images out of my head. Those pulsating roots, reaching out for the students, sucking them down with them.

Stop thinking, Andy! I shout it out as loud as possible inside my head.

We've got to wait it out, that's all. I don't know about the others, but my heart won't stop hammering and my hands have gone clammy. Have the footsteps moved away? I can't tell. A few minutes pass and I begin to think we might be safe. I force myself to take slow breaths in and out. It's supposed to relax you, but my adrenaline is pumped so high, it's not working.

Another minute passes. I open my mouth to suggest we get out of here and back to our houses as fast as possible, but I clamp it shut promptly as the door begins to creak open ominously. Our eyes widen with fear.

They're coming for us.

Chapter 11

I'm shrinking further and further down behind the sofa, as far as I can go. Jane has hidden her whole face inside the top of her hoodie, but Murk is in a squat position, like she's ready to leap out and defend us if the need arises. I sincerely hope it doesn't because I don't fancy her chances against a gang of Ravens wielding their super-human strength.

The door squeaks shut, and I clench my fists, nails digging into my palms. I should have followed Jane's lead and buried my head in my hoodie.

"We can talk in here," a voice says.

"Let's get organised." That was a different voice.

"Yeah, time we got the numbers down!" another one laughs.

Phew. It's not the guards come to haul us away. It's a group of students. But wait – what? *Time to get the numbers down?* Did he really say that?

Murk sidles to the edge of the sofa and peers around cautiously. She'd make a damn good spy. She edges back and mouths, "Five."

Five of them. Like us, the LNS, they're forming an alliance by the sounds of it. But their goals and our goals are different. They want to eliminate their competitors. We want to save everyone. And escape.

"Kill or be killed," one of them says.

I can't believe what I'm hearing. Everyone's been scared to sleep – fearing that someone might pull a pillow over their face and suffocate them – but we all figured we weren't allowed to actively take anyone out unless it's while playing the games. I tune back in to what the students are saying. They're talking about exactly that.

"Trust me, I'm 100 per cent sure we're allowed to do this."

"Yeah, no one's said that we can't take out the competition. The strongest and the smartest survive. This is a clever move."

No! No! No! This is a sick move, I want to shout at them. But grotesquely, it makes sense . . .

"So how do we do this, Adam?" one of them says.

"Watch the other competitors. The strongest ones are the ones we need to get rid of first, so we've got a better chance of winning the games. We'll pick them off one by one."

"And seize the chance to get rid of a few, when we see it. We can do it – as long as we stick together."

"You two are in Well House." That sounds like Adam again. He's definitely the ring-leader of this group. "Check out the competition there. We'll make a move as soon as you've identified the main threats to us."

"There's five of us. Let's make sure we're the last five standing."

"Let's do it!"

I hazard a quick peek over the sofa and see them high-fiving.

"Remember," a tall, dark-haired boy says, "the faster we get this done, the sooner the games end." That's Adam.

I duck back down and hear the door creaking open as they finally leave.

Just when I thought it couldn't possibly get any worse! This is the grim reality of our situation now. Murk looks at me. I know she's thinking the same. No more looking for answers, for clues, for anything! We need to focus on getting the hell out of this school.

We wait another minute or two to make sure they're gone before prising ourselves out of our hiding place.

"OK, our plan has to change," Murk says immediately. "You can be sure there's more alliances like that one and they're gunning for blood."

"I agree. I can't believe that they could actually go through with killing someone. They wouldn't really do it, would they? Do you know them, Murk?"

"Adam's a year ten. He's in my house – lucky me, eh! The others are year nines, I don't know them."

"You'd better watch your back if he's in your house, Murk," I warn her.

"Don't worry about me. But, yeah, those boys were deadly serious. They want to win. They want to live. And only five of us are going to have that privilege."

"We need to get word to the others," I say, practically hyperventilating with fear. "We need to get to the village and tell the police ASAP! We need to get out and we need to get out now!"

Jane is shaking her head. "No. I don't trust the police to do anything. They did nothing when my grandparents reported my aunty missing. Go ahead if you want. I'm staying."

"You can't," Murk insists.

"I have to! I don't have a choice."

Murk throws her hands up in the air with exasperation. "There's always a choice. You've just got to make the right one. You're not gonna help anyone by getting killed. Well House is being targeted first – that's your house!"

"Then I'll hide. They won't find me. I'm not their biggest threat there. Look at me." She points to her tiny frame. "You've got more to worry about, Murk. They'll come for you before they come for me."

"Argh!" I pace around the room. "What do we do? Please, Jane. I can't leave you here alone – you mean a lot to me." It just comes out without me thinking about how she'll take it. "If we go, we go together," I finish.

Jane looks as surprised at my admission as I am and her face softens. But then she gathers herself, her stubbornness back in force. "Andy, you know better than everyone else why I can't leave yet. And like Murk said, you've got a choice. I'm not forcing you to stay."

We're at loggerheads.

Murk finally breaks the heavily-charged atmosphere. "Listen, guys, we've got to remember we're on the same side," she reminds us. "I'm going back to my house. I'll get that stuff for you, Jane. We'll talk later, OK? Best we leave one by one." She heads to the door and inches it open. She peeks out and nods that it's all clear, and disappears into the corridor.

"Jane?" I start, reaching for her.

She walks past me to the door. "Don't, Andy. You know

why I've got to see the games through to the end. I want justice for my aunty." Then she's gone.

I want justice for her too. And for all the other kids who've lost their lives. But we have to be alive for that to happen.

***

I make my way back to Charter House. My thoughts are spiralling in a vortex of doom and gloom. It's exhausting constantly watching over your shoulder, eyes peeled and darting in every direction, hugging the walls of the buildings, shoulders hunched to make yourself inconspicuous. I'm surrounded by people who want to kill me.

Down the hall there are voices coming from the direction of the common room. I decide to avoid the area and head up to the dorm, hoping there's no one there. I need to regroup, sit down and think this through, but I spot my rucksack on the floor next to the bed, so first I pack it with essentials in case I need to make a quick getaway.

Only then do I prop my pillow up and sit on the bed. I don't bother taking my trainers off – same reason I can't allow myself to relax one iota. I've got to be ready to run. I silently thank my mum for these trainers. Thinking of my parents back home makes me want to cry. I was going to be the first one in the family to go to university. Dad went to a tech college – he's an engineer, and Mum went to nursing college, but neither of them got the chance to go to university. Those hopes were pinned on me. Looks as though my little brother will have to carry that torch for them.

But I'm not giving up yet.

I lean back on the pillow and feel the rustle of paper in

my pocket. It's the pages I ripped from the charter. I pull them out and read our names, with 'The Lost Name Society' written at the top.

Whatever happens, I've got to remember that we're stronger together. We need answers and we need them fast because there's no way we're going to be able to persuade Jane to leave. I look at the pages again. They each wrote their real name and then crossed it out – just the way I did in assembly. It suddenly hits me that there *is* something I can do. I can tear out all the charter pages, just like I did before. I can break Ms Merrybourne's hold! I push off the bed and head downstairs to the hall.

There it is. The glass cabinet with the charter returned to its place on the stand inside it. I glance around the hall. I'm alone. I open the glass door and reach for the book, but pull my hand back when I hear voices. I push the door to and step into the shadows beyond the cabinet, pressing myself flat against the wall. The voices head straight outside to the quad. I take a breath and return to the glass cabinet. Quickly, I open it and reach for the charter.

A red flame appears and it engulfs my hand. I stifle a cry as I snatch my hand back as fast as I can. I blow on my hand and then realise that it hasn't burnt me, but it won't allow me to tear any pages from it. There must be some kind of spell or enchantment to protect the book, which wasn't there when I ripped the pages out at assembly. They must have had to lift the spell to allow us to sign our names in it.

There goes that plan!

On the wall beside the charter, cast in shadow, there's

a plaque. The spotlight above it isn't working, so I use my phone torch. The latest entry on the plaque is the year 2000 and one of the winners was Seung-min Park.

Jane's aunty! But if she was one of the winners then why is she missing? Are *all* the winners missing? If so, what's happened to them?

My brain is doing somersaults trying to compute this new info. I run my eyes across to the first entry. It's dated 1675. That's the year that the school was established; its founding year. Does that mean that this ritual has been going on since the very beginning? That's 350 years! One Pentangle Prize Championship every twenty-five years.

My mind is reeling. I do the maths.

Fourteen Championships.

A hundred contestants in each championship.

Five winners.

So in total, if ninety-five died in each Championship, that's 1330 students. *Dead*!

Five winners per championship means seventy winners over the last 350 years. We know Jane's aunty is missing, but what of the other winners? What's happened to them?

I rummage in my pocket. I've still got Belle's pen. I pull out my charter pages and begin to write out the names of the previous winners, ending with the winners of 2000.

The safety of the dorm room upstairs beckons. I'm shattered and I should rest in case we're called for the next game, but I know I won't be able to. I need answers first and foremost, and there's only one place I'm going to find them. It means leaving the safety of the dorm behind and venturing out again. Where there are eyes everywhere, watching your every move, spying on you. I suppress the shudder of fear. *I've got this*, I tell myself.

I slip out of Charter House. I have to retrace my steps and get to the library.

Chapter 12

The map of the school is tucked in my pocket, but I don't need it as I've committed it to memory. One day, after I get out of here, I hope my brain eliminates it. That's one memory I don't want to be carrying around with me for ever. I avoid cutting through the centre Tangle, where there are a few groups of students milling about. Forming alliances, I guess. I don't blame them. I blame Ms Merrybourne.

Miraculously, I make it through to the corridor where the library is located without encountering any trouble. I breathe more easily. Murk pointed out where the library was but it's impossible to miss. It says 'LIBRARY' in big bold letters across the top of the arched wooden doors. I turn the brass handle and enter.

It's cavernous, panelled in dark wood, and the high vaulted ceilings are painted with frescos. There's muted light from soft spotlights. I wait a moment and listen – other students might have had the same idea and come here to find info. But it's silent. I might be alone in here, or I might not. It's better not to take a risk, so I avoid the central aisle and take a route down the bookshelves forming the side aisles.

Where do I start? My mobile is in my pocket, but it's pretty useless without Wi-Fi. I can't search anything on it. I've got to do this old-school style, as my dad would say. The charter might be the key, so that's what I have to look for info on: first Charter House and then the charter itself. I head deeper into the library, looking for the non-fiction section.

Further up, the library widens and the whole section at the rear looks like it's full of reference books. There are several bookcases with glass fronts to protect collections of ancient books. I slide one book case open and notice the books have weathered leather bindings holding together thick parchment-type paper. They're hand-written, but the cursive script is practically illegible and I can only make out words like 'and' and 'the'. I replace it and silently shout at the ceiling in frustration. I could spend a month in here and still not find what I'm looking for.

I walk further and notice that some aisles are labelled: 'GEOGRAPHY', 'SCIENCE', 'HISTORY'. *Finally!* But when I check out the history books, it's stuff we've done in school – Tudors and Stewarts, wattle and daub houses, the Industrial Revolution, the Transatlantic Slave Trade. I reach for a book on the Gunpowder Plot and remember a lesson at school about witchcraft in the Jacobean period. Back then, people were obsessed with witches, black magic and demonic possession. The paranoia led to accusations and even executions. I shove the book back quickly. My head is already spinning with the merry-go-round of weird stuff going on here and it definitely doesn't need the extra fuel.

I can't find a single book on the history of the school, never mind a book specifically about Charter House. I slump down on a stool, exhaustion oozing through every limb. The hellfire tree took it out of me and now I'm feeling the pain.

My head sinks into my hands. A shuffling noise breaks the silence, sending me into high alert. I hunch low on the stool, trying to gauge where it's coming from. Soft footsteps. Heading my way. I slide onto the floor, my back up against a bookcase, feeling trapped.

Then something hits me on the head and I yelp before jumping to my feet and charging for the main door. I'm halfway there when I realise that I must have just dislodged a book and that's what hit me over the head. I'm such an idiot! And on top of that, whoever is in here now definitely knows that I'm here too.

I'm trying to glance in every direction in the same split-second, looking for danger, for whoever else is hiding in here and might come for me. So I don't see the person I collide with until I've slammed into her and knocked her off her feet.

"B-Belle!" I stammer.

Her shocked expression quickly fades to stark relief. She shakes her head and sighs. "Just one time, Andy, just once, it would be good to meet up with you when you're looking where you're going." And then she smiles, which completely disarms me. "But if anyone was going to bump into me in this creepy place, I'm so glad it's you." She holds out her hand. "Help me up."

"Sorry, I got spooked. Running always seems the best option," I add lamely. No way am I going to tell her I got startled by a book landing on my head! "Did you find anything?"

"Not much. I was looking for info on the previous headteachers. There was one interesting fact though – they take the same title. All the heads were called *Merrybourne.* Weird, huh?"

"Are you serious? What does it mean?"

"No idea. I've been looking into the history behind the word 'Merrybourne'. 'Merry' is pretty easy, although I wouldn't call our head merry in any way. And there are lots of meanings for 'bourne': stream, limit, boundary, destination, goal. The village is called the same. But, listen to this – the word 'merry' is derived from the French '*mourir*' – dead. If you add in the 'bourne', it could mean born of the dead. And then someone disturbed me, so I didn't get any further." She mock-punches my arm playfully.

"At least I'm keeping you on your toes," I reply. "*Born of the dead* sounds like it's right out of a horror film."

"It does, you're right. It kind of feels like we're stuck inside a horror film! And I should have scouted out a better hiding place before burying my head in the books. What were you looking for before you got freaked out?"

"Anything on the history of the school charter, but I didn't get far either. Let's stick together in here," I suggest. "We can take it in turns to keep look-out."

We spend the next hour trawling through the library, opening and shutting hundreds of books. I can't find a single thing about the previous winners – no information about them at all. Not even photos.

"You'd think they'd celebrate the winners," Belle says. "It's a big deal winning one of these championships!"

"And they always take photos of winners. Wouldn't they say what university they went to – that's the whole point of the games, isn't it? And yet there's no info on the Pentangle Prize anywhere."

"Or if there is, we need longer to find it. Let's keep looking. It's not like there's any place we need to be," Belle suggests.

I'm dreaming of my bed and how I need to lie down and shut my eyes before we get called to play the next game. But she's right. I rub my eyes and sigh heavily.

***

Another hour passes and we regroup with nothing more to add to what little we know. Belle's easy to chat to, and we sit for a while. It almost feels normal, except for the reason why we're in the library. It's not to do our homework, or read a book, it's to find information that might save our lives. I summon up the courage to ask her about herself.

"So what's your story, Belle?"

"You really wanna know?"

"I do. I can't figure out if you're Asian like me."

"Haha, wrong continent!" Belle's tinkling laughter fills the air. "My parents adopted me from an orphanage in Sudan when I was a baby." She chews her lip before adding, "They were in a rock band which did pretty well back in the day, so they decided to adopt a poor African baby."

"They're not Sudanese?"

"No, they're English."

"Oh." A lame response, but I don't know what to say.

"It's OK. My parents had a wild time when they were younger. But when they retired from that life and adopted me, everything changed. They started growing their own veg on their allotment, or trying, and making sure I was the happiest little kid in the world." She laughs softly. "I even had the most gorgeous dun-coloured pony. I called him Button.

My parents are great, you know. They're laid-back hippies, really. I'm not like them at all. I couldn't wait to go to boarding school. And now I can't wait to get home to them. Ironic, huh? What about you?"

"I never lived in India. My parents came over to the UK because they were offered jobs, so I was born here. And same – I couldn't wait to get here either, and now all I want is to go home. Don't think they would ever have imagined that me using Andy as my name might have saved my life."

"Yeah, that's true. Trixibelle would have been dead by now. Lucky for me, Belle has got lots of good friends watching her back."

She counts me as a good friend, and I feel a flush of warmth. "And lucky for me I caught you on camera on my first day," I reply.

We sit in silence for a while, until we're both yawning madly.

"I'm calling it, Andy," Belle says, pulling out a chair from a table and sitting. She tilts the chair back on two legs, her head resting on the wall behind. "The bell will go for dinner soon and we haven't had a chance to rest yet." She rubs her ribs, grimacing.

"Still painful?" I ask.

"Close call." She shudders. "But I'll heal." She reaches up with her arms, stretching. "OK, shall we head?"

"Hey, wait a minute." My eyes are drawn to the noticeboard behind her. There's a photo of a man wearing a robe and an ornate chain around his neck. I go closer for a better look. "Councillor Jim Simmonds," I read out. The name rings a bell.

"The current mayor of Merrybourne village," Belle says.

I take out the charter pages and read through the list of the names of past winners. "There it is!" I stab the paper with my finger. "He's got the same surname as one of the past winners – from the 1700s!"

"Hmm. It might not mean anything. 'Simmonds' isn't the most uncommon name."

"It's possible though, isn't it? Like Jane and her aunty are related. And all the heads share the same name."

Belle chews her lip thoughtfully. "I'll give you that. Anything is possible."

"Me and Jane and Murk were headed here earlier, but we thought we were being followed by Ravens so we hid. It turned out to be another group of students. They were plotting. Our deaths."

Belle's chair hits the floor with a slam as she sits up. "What?"

"Yeah. They're forming alliances to eliminate anyone who poses a threat to them. They're keeping a list of students from each of the houses. It's no holds barred when it comes to winning this competition. They're going to hit Well House first and take out the strongest. And that's just the group we overheard. There'll be others planning the same thing."

Piers and his gang will be among them, and that makes me very afraid. What was I thinking about trying to get any sleep in my dorm with Piers on the loose?

"Just when you think it can't get any worse," Belle says. "If I went missing, my parents would tear down every brick in this place looking for me."

I lean forwards. “And they wouldn’t find you. They never found Jane’s aunty.”

“So we need a new plan.”

“Yes – we need to get out. Fast.”

“Sounds like a plan to me. We might all be dead before we find any answers to what’s going on here.”

“We get out, and find Mayor Simmonds. He’s in charge in the village, he’ll help us.”

“Do we go to the police?” Belle says. “Jane said they did nothing much when her aunty went missing.”

“And that’s the other thing,” I say. “Somehow we have to persuade Jane to come with us. She’ll have to.” I hope.

“And then there’s the other thing,” Belle says.

“What thing?”

“Surviving the next game.”

It’s always about that.

Chapter 13

"Through the woods, that's our best bet," Ford says. His dinner plate is piled high as usual. He must have an incredible metabolism. But then I suppose he's an athlete. "I don't know when we should try it."

"Night-time, obvs," Murk says. "It's too risky in the day-time."

"Yeah, we'd be spotted too easily," I add. "Where's the closest spot to the woods?"

"Around the back of the school, near the tennis courts," Ford says. "Trees line the path out to the courts, and then the woods begins at the far end. There's a cabin where spare racquets and balls are stored, which might come in handy if we need to hide. It's never locked."

"Can't imagine the guards will be patrolling that far out," Belle says. "Do we go tonight?"

In the end we decide it's too risky without an escape route.

"I'll do a reccy tonight," Ford says. "I'll take my tennis racquet with me in case I get seen – I'm often out there practicing my serve. It'll be useful as a weapon too if any of the other students come at me."

Only Jane has remained silent throughout the exchange. Nothing we've said has made her change her mind. We tried throughout the evening, but she is adamant. She has made her decision. She's staying. Come what may. And I am totally gutted.

Jane might be right in that it's a total waste of time trying to plan an escape. But hope is the only thing we have going for us. I have to win her round and help her see that.

"Staying is like giving up," I tell Jane. "And I'm not ready to give up."

"What happened to trying to find answers and saving everyone? Do you really think we can outwit Ms Merrybourne or outrun the guards?" Jane's eyes flash angrily. "You're all deluded."

Belle gives her a steady look. "Nothing wrong with trying, Jane. I'm not going to die here. None of us are. We're going to get out." She says it with such certainty and then spreads her fingers on one hand out and places them on her chest.

We follow suit, in solidarity. Fist-bumping would draw unwanted attention, and *that* we do not need. I see Jane's hand tentatively rising to join our salute, and I smile encouragingly at her. She's one of us – no matter what she decides to do.

We part ways to return to our houses at the end of the fraught dinner.

***

I creep into my dorm much later that evening. It's silent apart from the rise and fall of breathing and the soft snore of one of the students. They're sleeping! How is that possible when the executioner's axe is swinging right above their heads with such glee?

My bed beckons, but there's no way I will be able to sleep. My insides are a jumble of knotted nerves, and adrenaline is fizzing through every clenched muscle. Will's empty bed opposite me is another grim reminder that death stalks us – at the games, in the school grounds and buildings – even here in the dorm, which should feel safe. I'm convinced that someone will come for me tonight, and that person is most likely to be Piers, or one of his minions sent to do his dirty work.

And then the loud crackling of the tannoy system and the blast of the bell resound around the room. I lurch off the bed, still fully clothed, still in my trainers, and realise that I fell asleep after all. And I'm still alive, but that heavy crackling of the tannoy only means one thing. My pulse beats faster as I wait for the disembodied voice to make the announcement.

"The next game is due to begin in one hour. After breakfast please make your way to Well House. Dress code is your Merrybourne tracksuit," the voice announces. "Do not be late."

There are groans from some of the students. Others are silent. I rub the sleep from my eyes, and note how many kids are sporting bruises and scratches, which is bad enough. But it's their dead eyes that get to me. It's like someone has sucked their souls right out of them.

Well House is Jane's house. I'm pretty confident that the gang we overheard in the common room yesterday wouldn't have perceived her as a strong threat and would have left her alone. Maybe their planning was all bravado. I mean, it's not easy sneaking around the school, what with the Ravens being everywhere. Killing someone in cold blood without attracting attention would be even harder.

In the common room, a breakfast spread has been laid

out again. I have zero appetite, but I need to eat. Whatever the game is today and the challenges we might face, I'll need every ounce of energy and then some. I quickly chomp through a couple of boiled eggs and swallow them down with glugs of milk, trying not to gag. I love eggs, just not boiled ones. Soft, buttery scrambled eggs the way my mum makes them are the best. The pang of homesickness hits me like a punch to my gut. It's accompanied by a bucket-load of self-pity. I shove the self-pity down deep because feeling sorry for myself takes away my edge. And that might get me killed.

It's best not to think of home, or my mum, dad and Vik either. As I head out of Charter House, the only thought in my mind is the hope that the rest of the Lost Name Society survived the night too. And that we survive this game.

Students are already making their way towards Well House. I take a moment. Leaning against the wall of Charter House, I watch them. They're quiet as anything. A lone bird trills from close by, but its song stutters and fades. Even the birds are struggling to find their voice here.

I join the others, following the paths that lead to the centre Tangle, lined, as ever, with cloaked guards. And from there we make our way to Well House quad. I shiver. It's September but there's a chill to the morning air; I wish my standard Merrybourne issue trackie was fleece lined.

Before I know it, Well House is looming large in front of me. We file into its quad, my eyes drawn to the huge well at the centre – it looks ancient with its mossy stone walls. Ms Merrybourne stands beside it, dressed in another form-fitting, snake-like dress.

She beckons us. "Come closer, my dears."

I follow the remaining contestants over to the well and we cluster around it. I'm guessing the next game isn't going to be as easy as drawing water from the well!

"Can you see down the well?" she asks us.

I peer over gingerly, wondering what the trap is, and whether one of my peers will take advantage of the situation and launch me over into it. The interior walls of the well are covered in green algae and slime, and then it plunges into an inky-black darkness. I can see down the well just fine, but I can't see the bottom of it. Is that where the losers end up? At the bottom of the well?

"You will need to find your way *out* of the well to win this challenge," Ms Merrybourne says.

The murmur of voices around me rises to a crescendo. It's the same question, repeated again and again. 'Did she say *out* of the well? What does that mean?' When the big screen flickers on above us, revealing a maze-like map, all becomes clear. My heart starts pounding. The only thing I hate more than dark, enclosed spaces, are dark, enclosed spaces that are under the ground.

"Silence!" Ms Merrybourne claps her hands. "This game will test your non-verbal reasoning. Listen carefully: there are a series of underground tunnels down there. To find the correct route out you must solve multiple-choice shape and pattern problems at each juncture. Only the correct route will lead you to the exit through the well."

This is horrific. And then it gets worse as Ms Merrybourne continues.

"Oh, did I mention that there's a time limit? Not the usual, dear students, but something else. The water level will be your timer.

"The water in the tunnels will rise and keep rising. So make sure you get out as fast as you can, my dears." Ms Merrybourne beams at us.

This is a whole different level of horrific.

The Ravens move in and funnel us towards different corners of the quad where there are tables laid out with torches. I glance around me but I don't see any of the LNS. We've been shunted to different sections. Beyond the tables, gaping holes suddenly open up in the ground. We're pushed into them unceremoniously and stumble down the stone steps. Kids fight their way past me as I fumble with my torch, trying to find the on button, and in my haste, I slip. I clutch at the wall to stop myself falling down the steps. Above us, the hole has closed up, plunging us into darkness, sealing us in.

I squeeze my eyes shut and suppress a cry of fear as the walls close in on me. The only way out is through the well. And I have to find it. There is no other option. I manage to switch on my torch and force myself to move. Dots of light appear from bobbing torches on the steps as students switch on their torches. They're moving fast. No one is wasting any time.

At the bottom of the steps the water is below my ankle. I slosh through the tunnel, shouting out for Murk, for Belle, for Jane and Ford, hoping one of them will hear me. Somehow I have to find them, but will they hear me when everyone's yelling for their friends? Panicked voices are echoing all around me.

The tunnel opens out to a wider space. Three tunnels branch out from it. I shout out my friends' names into each of them until I hear my name shouted back. It sounds like Murk's voice. I head up the tunnel as fast as I can. At the end of the tunnel a light is blinking on and off, guiding me. I reach the end and throw my arms around Murk in relief. That's two of us.

"Ford's coming down that tunnel," she tells me. "No idea where the rest are."

I glance towards the tunnel and see that Ford's got Belle with him, which leaves Jane.

"We've got to find Jane," I say.

"OK, we haven't tried those two tunnels. We'll split into two groups and meet back here," Belle suggests. "Me and Ford will take that tunnel," she says, nodding towards the tunnel on the right.

"OK," I mumble, a little upset she didn't pick me. I guess it's because there's history with Ford. I try not to think about it.

"Keep a look out for the puzzles. I haven't seen a single one," Ford adds. "Luckily, the water doesn't seem to be rising yet."

I'm not so sure about that. The water was not quite ankle-deep when I stepped into the tunnel. Now it's definitely at my ankle. I glance up. The roof of the tunnel is about a foot above my head. Will the water rise up to the top?

"I don't trust them. They could flood this place in seconds for all we know. We've got to hurry."

"Re-group here in three minutes," Ford says, already

heading for one of the tunnels. "If we don't find her, we can't waste any more time."

"We're not leaving anyone behind!" I shoot back. No way am I leaving Jane in this hellhole.

Murk turns and sprints for our tunnel. She does a quick sidestep as a student is about to collide with her. He trips and sprawls in front of me. I reach out a hand to help him up and realise it's Marco from my house. His eyes are wide with fear.

"Stick with us," I tell him. He doesn't seem to hear me. He launches himself up and races off. "Marco!" I yell. "Come back!" He's gone.

I hope he'll be OK.

Murk has moved on already, calling out Jane's name. She's got way ahead of me. I hear someone shouting back and hope it's Jane, but there is an echo of voices calling and shouting in the tunnel system. Then Murk is turning back towards me.

"She's there. I'll get the others," she shouts on her way past me.

I reach the end and find Jane, waiting. She hurls her arms around me, and her face buries in my chest, her body shaking with relief. I hold her tightly, realising just how pleased I am to see her – just how much I care. "It's OK, Jane."

She steps back. "Sorry, I can't bear it down here. I was so afraid I was on my own . . . that you'd left me."

The panic to find everyone has driven my own phobia of dark, enclosed spaces out of my head. It's strange what real fear and the need to survive can do to you. "No way were we leaving any of our group behind," I reassure her.

"That's good to know. After dinner last night, I thought

you lot were going to try and escape and abandon me here."

"We would have taken you with us – even if I had to drag you away kicking and screaming."

"It might come to that. If we don't die down here first. The water's rising," she says.

It's above my ankle. "How long do you think we have?"

She shrugs. "Who knows?" She peers down the tunnel. "I think that's the others coming."

Once we've re-grouped, we have to decide which way to go. Ahead of us are another three tunnels.

"Flip a coin?" Murk suggests.

"No need. I think I know the way out," Jane says. "Last night I snuck into the housemaster's office and found a map. I wasn't sure what it was at first, but then I realised that it had to be a network of tunnels. I memorised it as best I could, and then remembered my phone. The camera app still works, so I took photos."

"Oh my god, Jane, you're the true MVP!" Murk hugs her.

"But we still have to solve the puzzles," Belle says. "Non-verbal reasoning isn't my thing."

"I'm pretty good at those," Jane says. "Coding camp – best summer camp I ever went on."

"Good job we found you then." Ford grins. "This game is right up your street."

Murk clutches my arm and I turn to her. "Murk?" She's staring down one of the tunnels.

"What is that?" she whispers. She heads into the tunnel cautiously.

We begin to follow more slowly – everyone except Ford,

who says, "There's a weird light down there and I don't like the look of it."

I move closer to the source of the light. "It's – it's . . . I'm not sure," I stammer.

Large tendrils of what look like a plant of some kind are wafting in the breeze. How can there be a breeze down here? It's cold and it's damp, and without the torches, it's pitch black. There's no way plants can survive down here without natural light. But this one is somehow very much alive, and it's pulsating with some kind of warm red-orange light. There's nothing natural about it; it's almost other-worldly. Yet I'm drawn to it. I need to see it close up. I edge around Murk to get a better look.

"Can you hear that?" Belle murmurs as she follows me. "It's calling us, isn't it? We should get closer to it. There might be a puzzle beyond it."

Both of us are moving towards it, drawn by whatever hold it is exerting. It's a wondrously strange thing, all alone down here in the darkness. It wants us to get closer, it wants us to touch it.

Murk yanks us both back, shaking us out of our weird reverie. "What are you doing?" she hisses. "It's dangerous – look what it's making you do!" She draws us away from it with a shudder.

"Well?" Ford asks.

"That thing was pulling us towards it. Don't know what the hell it is. I suggest we avoid going any further down that tunnel. Unless," she turns to Jane, "it's the way out. Please say it's not."

Jane gets her phone out and zooms in on a section of the map. She's trying to figure out where we are. I don't know how she's able to work it out – it's not like that weird plant will be marked on it, and the tunnels are a maze.

"Um. No pressure, Jane," Ford begins, "but the water's up to our shins now."

Chapter 14

"Got it! It's that one." Jane points to the middle tunnel and we collectively breathe a sigh of relief. Getting any closer to that strange plant-like creature would have been way too dangerous.

The water is deeper as we slosh through the tunnel, and the noises coming from up ahead are ominous. It doesn't take us long to work out that a fight has broken out. And we're headed right towards it. Half way through the tunnel, two students dart past us, dripping wet.

"Don't go that way! They're going for everyone!" one of them shouts. Blood is dripping into his eye from a gash on his forehead.

There are five of us against however many might be waiting for us at the end of the tunnel, but still. The last thing any of us wants is to get into a brawl.

"Stay with us," I tell him, but he's gone. The shouting from up ahead gets louder. "Is there any other way, Jane?" I ask.

Jane peers at her phone. "We could try down there." She points at a narrow opening off the tunnel. "I'm not sure though. Looks like it might be a dead-end."

"Then it's a waste of time," Ford says, dismissing it. "Find another way."

He's really getting on my nerves now. Jane's trying to do

her best – and if it wasn't for her and the map of the tunnels we'd be totally lost. On top of that, he's awful to Murk, but Belle doesn't seem to notice.

"We'll give it a go, dead-end or not," I say, and head down the opening. I hear Ford cursing behind me, but everyone follows. This route has the feel of a cave rather than a properly- formed tunnel. I can reach out and touch the rough stone roof easily. Then I reach the end.

Jane was right. It's a dead-end.

"What did I tell you?" Ford groans. "We've wasted time!"

I turn and glare at him. "We had to try something!"

"Hey, guys, wait." Murk is pointing her torch at something carved into the wall. "Is that what I think it is?"

"Yes!" I punch the air with relief.

In front of us is the first non-verbal reasoning puzzle we've come across.

"'Find the shape or pattern which completes the puzzle. Press the right one to get to the next level'," Belle reads.

"So the answer is a, b, c or d," Murk says. "I always hated multiple choice!"

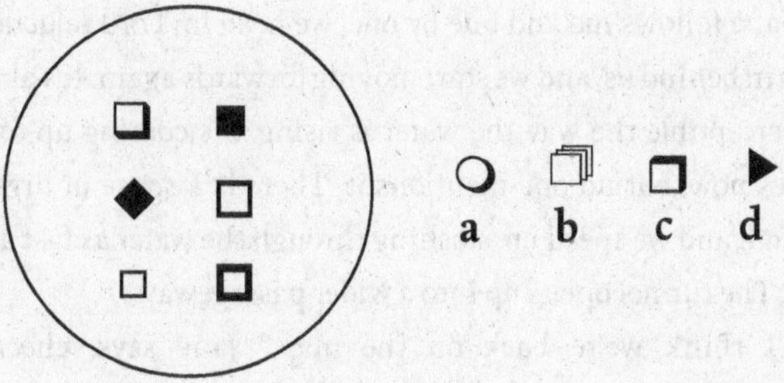

The tunnel is dark, but the puzzle is illuminated with a softly-glowing greenish tint. We stare at the patterns, trying to make connections between them. Meanwhile, the water level is rising fast.

Jane moves in front of me and reaches out. "It's that one," she says, and presses the 'c' before we can stop her. I don't even want to think about what might happen if it's the wrong answer. Does a barrier come down, trapping us while the cave floods and drowns us?

"You should have consulted with the rest of us first," Ford says.

"It's the right answer!" Jane snaps, just as the wall slides open, revealing an even darker tunnel. "It's a square!"

The light from our torches barely penetrates the gloom.

"It wouldn't open if it wasn't the right answer," I say.

"Or it's the wrong answer and we're going to be trapped inside there," Belle says.

No one takes a step inside the tunnel as Belle's words sink in.

I make the first move. "I'm going to trust Jane," I say, and step inside the tunnel. "Anyone coming?"

Jane follows me and one by one, we head in; Ford reluctantly falls in behind us, and we start moving forwards again. It's almost imperceptible the way the water is rising. It's coming up to our knees now, but no one mentions it. There is a sense of urgency though and we speed up, sloshing through the water as fast as we can. The tunnel opens up into a wider passageway.

"I think we're back on the map," Jane says, checking the photo on her phone. "That way next," she says, pointing.

We surge ahead, our trackies drenched, our trainers soaked with slimy water, and we don't hear or see the danger until it's too late. An arm whips out and smacks Belle across the head. It was badly aimed and only just clips her, but it has made her lose her footing and she stumbles into the water. More hands appear and try to seize us. I bat the hands away blindly. We can't see who it is in the darkness. I flash my torch up to see Jane ducking, but Belle has been caught and is being dragged away. Murk reacts fast and lashes out at the arm holding Belle.

There are five of them. Two of them get hold of Ford and start punching him. Ford is strong and fit, but the odds are stacked against him. I'm not a fighter. I've never, ever thrown a punch. I don't like rugby, so I've never even tackled anyone, but two against one isn't fair. I shove my torch in my pocket and go for one of them, but Murk pushes me aside.

"Get behind with Belle and Jane. And shine your torch so I can see what I'm doing!" she screams as she launches herself at the plotters.

I pull my torch out and add it to the light from Belle and Jane's torches. It's quite a spectacle the way Murk and Ford fight off our attackers. They're working together, for a change. Ford's fitness and stamina is too much for his opponent, and he's soon floored him. Murk is a fury of kicks and punches and she deflects everything coming at her with ease. I'm definitely taking up jiu jitsu – if I ever make it out of here alive.

Our attackers soon scarper and we can breathe for a moment. There's no time to lose, though, as ahead of us is our next challenge and this puzzle looks harder.

“So that’s why they didn’t want anyone coming down here,” Murk says.

“No one wants anyone else to solve the puzzles and get through to the next level,” I mutter. “Same as in the tree. Everyone is out for themselves.”

“But none of them could solve the puzzle or else they wouldn’t have been standing here guarding it,” Belle says.

“It’s not that hard,” Jane says, stepping forwards to press the button.

“Don’t press the answer yet!” Ford says. “It’s got to be right.”

“OK, but we’re losing time,” Jane snaps. “Look at it carefully.”

I do, but I still don’t get it.

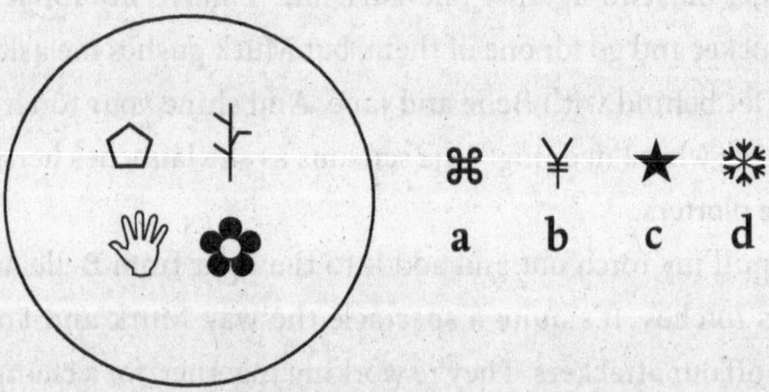

The others focus on it too, trying to make sense of it. The tunnel is dark and the strange green glow coming off the lit-up display is disorientating.

“It’s c!” I shout, suddenly seeing it.

Jane nods. “The items in the circle all have five ends. ‘C’ is the only option that matches the trend.” She hits ‘c’, and the wall grinds open, revealing another tunnel. We waste no time and plough through it. The water level has risen again, and it's freezing cold, penetrating through our clothes. It seems to rise every time we solve a puzzle, I've noticed. I don't want to die down here. *Please let me not die here*, I repeat like a mantra.

How many more puzzles do we have to solve before we get to the well?

We're struggling to wade through the water. It's reached our waists, and if it rises any further, we're going to be in deep trouble. We can't move as fast through it either, so our progress is slower. My teeth chatter with the cold. Who built these tunnels? And why? What kind of sick mind would devise this devious system of torture for kids?

Four tunnels open up in front of us.

"Which way now, Jane?" Belle asks.

"Um." Jane is consulting the map, but the way she's turning it around and around makes me very worried. "The well is so close," she says, sounding anything but certain. "There are a couple of routes, but I can't work out which one is best."

Belle peers over her shoulder at the map. "Let's try that one first. The other one is longer. What do you think?"

"OK." Jane still sounds uncertain, but she points the way.

No one needs reminding that the water level has now reached above our waists. With Murk leading, we take the tunnel Jane points to. We've barely gone any distance when we hear someone yelling, "Hey! So good to see you guys! Hurry up. We're waiting for you!"

Murk sloshes to an abrupt stop and swivels around, the whites of her eyes luminous in the dark. "Piers is up ahead," she says tersely. "That's his voice. And you can be sure that he won't let us pass."

"We'll have to take the other route. There have got to be more ways out of here. Keep up!" Ford urges, ploughing back down the tunnel.

We're close behind Ford as we tread through the deep water. Piers's voice floats sinisterly behind us, followed by raucous laughter. It echoes in the tunnel and sounds like a pack of hyenas has joined him. He really doesn't care if we die.

My torch starts to flicker. *No!* The battery must be dying. Then it starts to blink off and on, until the light is so weak I can barely see anything.

It goes off and I'm plunged into darkness. I panic, feeling the walls closing in on me. I gasp for breath. The water is so cold I can't even feel my feet. All I can hear is Piers's disembodied voice, echoing and reverberating through the tunnel.

I've lagged behind everyone. I can barely see the glimmer of their torches now. I know they'll wait for me to catch up. Won't they? What if their torches are dying too? Without light, we'll definitely die down here. No one will ever find our bodies.

I have to stop myself from thinking that way. I'll only die if I stand still, so I have to move. I take a step and then another, forcing myself to focus on wading through the water and not on the debilitating thoughts screeching through my head. I go faster and faster, practically swimming, until I reach the others.

"Everyone, turn your torches off!" I scream as loud as I can. "We need to conserve the batteries. Except you, Ford, as you're at the front. And hold hands." Belle's torch is flickering too. They follow my command realising it won't be long before we're plunged into darkness and then we'll never find our way out.

Ford leads us into the second tunnel. It's so narrow we have to turn sideways and the uneven ground makes us lose our footing several times. We clutch each other's hands hard. The water level is almost at our chests. It's icy cold. I can feel the panic emanating from the others.

"There's another puzzle!" Ford yells.

"It'd better lead to the well, otherwise . . ." Murk leaves the rest unsaid.

The puzzle glows with the same eerie green light as the others. After the echoes of voices and screams and yelling, and Piers's laughter, it's suddenly too quiet. Only our heavy breathing and the sound of trickling water breaks the silence. All eyes are on the puzzle, and it's harder than the previous ones. I can't make head nor tail of it.

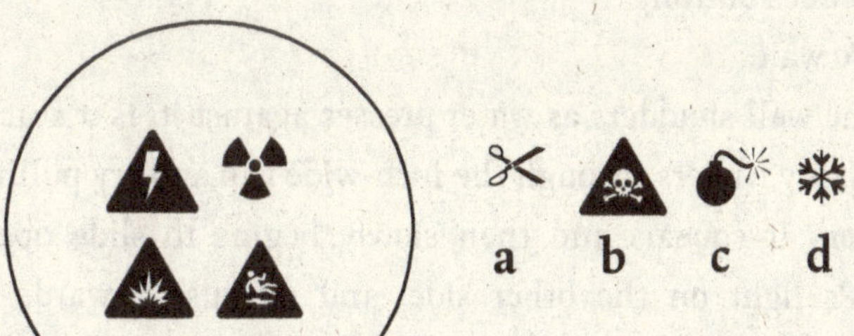

We're talking all at once, trying to work it out aloud, but none of us are sure. Only Jane has remained silent. We each reach a different answer. "Which one?" I shout in frustration.

“It’s this one.” Jane steps forwards. She pauses before pressing it. “In the circle, all the symbols are hazard signs: electrocution, fire, ice, radiation warning. If you look at the possible answers, they’re all dangerous things, but only one of them is a hazard sign that warns of danger in the same way that the ones in the circle do – so it’s ‘b’. Get it?” she checks with us.

“Makes sense,” Belle says. “But if it’s a warning of danger, does that mean we shouldn’t press it?”

It’s a good point, and I can almost hear everyone thinking this one through.

“Nah, we’re definitely overthinking it,” Ford says. “It’s the right answer.”

“Press it, Jane, otherwise you’ll be underwater soon,” Murk adds. Jane is the shortest in our group, and Murk is not wrong. The water level is nearly reaching Jane’s collarbone.

Jane takes a deep breath and pushes the skull and crossbones button.

We wait.

The wall shudders as water presses against it. Is it stuck? I push my fingers through the inch-wide gap and try pulling it open. It squeals and then slowly begins to slide open. There’s light on the other side, and we rush towards it, finally spying the walls of the well. We couldn’t see anything this far down from above the well before the game began, but inset in the walls of the well are stone steps leading upwards, to safety. Jane goes first, and we race up them, slipping and sliding on the slimy, mossy stone, even as the water is rising up the well.

We reach the top, clamber over the walls of the well and fall out onto the ground, our chests heaving as we pant for breath. It takes us a few minutes to realise that we were probably the last ones out. No one else can make it out of the well – not unless they're good at holding their breath. I glance around the quad.

There are fifteen other students, soaking wet and exhausted like us. That's it. No one else. Adam and his band of plotters from the common room are here. No surprise, Piers and his lot have made it. He gives me a look that seems to say, "I'll get you next time." I have no doubt he'll try. He almost got us today. A few more minutes and we wouldn't have made it.

That means there are twenty of us left in total, and still two more games to play.

"Those two who attacked me down there," Ford says, his voice hushed. "Luke and Andrew, they were my friends. We used to hang out, you know, and they were cool. Did you see their eyes?"

Murk nods. "They wanted to eliminate us. Some mates they turned out to be!"

Ford shrugs and looks away. "Doesn't matter now. They didn't make it."

Belle rubs Ford's arm. "It's the games. That's what forced them to act like that. Anyway, it's lucky for us that you're on our team. No way we would have made it out alive if it wasn't for you."

"Murk saved our lives, too," I say. "And we'd have been completely lost without Jane." With all eyes suddenly on me

I add, "What I mean is, we make a really great team. I'm grateful we have each other's backs."

Jane offers a tight-lipped smile while Belle and Murk nod in agreement. Ford's features have softened, and I can tell that even he's relieved to have this alliance.

Cold and exhausted, we wait for Ms Merrybourne to make her usual appearance, all chirpy that we managed to survive the game, and with no thought for the ones who died. But she doesn't show up. Instead, the guards tell us to return to our houses and get cleaned up.

We rise sluggishly to our feet, and as we're being herded out of Well House quad, I overhear one of the Ravens saying to another, ". . . the feeding."

I strain to catch more of what's being said, but the guards move away.

'*The feeding*'.

What does that mean? The ice-cold shiver racing down my spine is nothing to do with my wet clothes.

Chapter 15

We leave Well House quad, catching our breath, wondering what's next. The Ravens are receding into the background, leaving us alone. Just in case any of them are in earshot, I lower my voice. "I overheard something. Not sure what it means, but one of the Ravens was talking about 'the feeding'."

The others look puzzled.

"That doesn't sound good," Belle says, chewing her lip. "'The feeding' doesn't sound like the Ravens going off to have their lunch, that's for sure."

Murk's hands fly to her cloud of hair. "Oh, no! You know that creepy plant-like thing we saw down one of the tunnels? You know what it reminded me of? The roots of that monster tree at Oak House. They were exactly the same, weren't they?"

"Maybe," I say. "There were definitely strange vibes coming from it. Kind of hypnotic. I remember feeling the need to get closer to it."

"It was humming, or making a sound," Belle agrees. "I wanted to get closer to it too."

"Good job you didn't!" Murk said. "I'm sure it was waiting for us to get close enough so it could latch onto us, suck us in, or . . . feed off us."

"That's . . ." Ford pauses. "Possible, I guess."

We know Ford was about to say it was a ridiculous idea. But we've seen the stranger than stranger things that have been happening here; it's not so ridiculous. Not one bit.

"We all saw the roots of the tree swallowing up the students that fell. It took them with it when it disappeared back underground," Jane adds.

"Well, whatever it's doing, I think it's making the spell stronger," Murk says, "'cos everyone's still controlled by someone, or something. Apart from us."

"I'm in Oak House, so I can investigate the tree tonight," Belle offers.

"Too dangerous," I say, shaking my head.

"I agree," Ford says. "We need to focus on one thing – breaking out of here tonight. With only twenty contenders left in the games, I don't fancy our chances of survival. You saw the others. Tough lot to beat."

"I'm not losing anything by taking a look and seeing if I can discover something that might help us," Belle insists.

"We'll go together. Right now," Murk suggests. "Don't hang out too close together. Make it look casual, OK? Like we're drying off our clothes in the sunshine before heading to our dorms."

The sun is shining, but I can't feel its warmth through my stinking, dripping clothes. I want to go back and change, but I'm desperate to find out what's going on with the roots of the Oak House tree and whether it has anything to do with 'the feeding'.

We head out of Well House quad, through the Tangle,

and make our way to Oak House. There are a few Ravens around, but they're chatting among themselves. I guess their thinking is the game would have exhausted us so much that any thought of escape or dissent is going to be far from our minds for a good while.

I'm not sure I can take another night, much less another game, in this hellhole. As if reading my mind, Ford says, "Whatever happens, we go tonight. Be ready. We leave our stuff behind – no way we can carry anything that might slow us down."

"Yeah, stealth and speed," Murk adds.

"And a whole lot of luck," I add. "How did scouting the tennis courts go? Any chance we can get out that way?"

"I didn't see a single Raven there, so it's our best bet. There's a shed near the courts. We can meet up behind it."

"Take a circuitous route and make sure you're not followed. If you sense someone following, pretend you're out for a walk, go back to your house and sneak out later and take a different route. Memorise the map of the school and the grounds. There's one in each house," Murk says.

She is definitely spy material.

"How long do we wait for each other?" Belle asks. "How long before those who make it to the shed first decide that they can't wait any longer?"

"We wait until we're all there," I say adamantly.

"Until dawn breaks?" Belle persists. "Will we definitely all wait for each other?"

"Yes! I'm not leaving you behind, Belle," I say to reassure her.

"You'll be leaving *me* behind." Jane's tone is sad.

"No, you're coming with us, Jane. There's no point staying if you're here on your own," I tell her.

"I came here on my own," she says, her eyes flashing challengingly at me.

I'm taken aback at the vehemence in her voice. "But you've seen how the games work now. We need each other to survive them."

"You forget how much I've already given up! I had to keep my real name a secret and use *Jane*. That's not me! I even had to hide that I was coming here from my mum – and I never lie to her. So everything that makes me *me* I've hidden. My whole identity! Don't you get it?"

I hate to say it, but if it changes her mind then I have to. "You won't find out anything about your aunty if you're dead, Jane."

She glares daggers at me. "You promised you'd help."

"If we get out and find someone to help us—"

"Leave with the others," Jane says. "With Belle and everyone else," she adds under her breath as she turns away.

What? I'm not sure what's just happened. She feels I've let her down, but there's something more. Did she expect me to stay because she feels closer to me than the others? Maybe. I know I made that promise, but that was before we knew the extent of the madness of Ms Merrybourne and her macabre games.

The rest of the LNS try to persuade Jane, try to get her to change her mind, but to no avail. Jane is determined to stay.

"Jane," I begin again.

"Not now," she says wearily.

We've reached Oak House, but as soon as we enter its quad, we stop in our tracks. The tree stump is there in the middle of the quad with a cluster of guards surrounding it. Belle motions us to move nearer using the high hedges as cover. We creep around the quad, keeping low, our footsteps light, until we're close enough to see.

Ms Merrybourne is there. She's sitting on the stump, but it's no longer just a tree stump. It cups and curls around her, surrounding her like a throne. The strange red-orange roots of the tree are wrapped around her. No – wait. I think they're actually *attached* to her. They're writhing languidly across her, and she's smiling with her eyes half closed as though she's in a weird half-conscious dreamy sleep-like state.

Belle gasps. Jane raises a finger to her lips, telling her to keep quiet. This is the last place we want to be caught.

Then I see what caused Belle to gasp like that. All around Ms Merrybourne are the tree roots, but intertwined within the oranges and reds of the ghastly roots are bodies – lots of them. I hold on to the hedge and press my eyes to the gap.

What I see makes me clamp my hand over my mouth to stop myself from crying out. It's Will. His body is wrapped inside the tree roots. Is he actually dead? He must be. I know he is. I couldn't hold on to him in the tree and I saw him fall with my own eyes. But if there's even a small chance he's alive, can I save him? I have to try.

I half move, but Murk grabs my arm and forces me back.

She's seen the faces of the bodies too.

"There's nothing you can do," she whispers ever so softly. "The Ravens will take you and throw you at the roots, and you'll end up like your friend."

I glance at the other bodies and recognise more faces. It's the students who didn't survive the previous games, the ones who fell in the vipers' nest, the ones who fell from the tree, and the ones who never made it out of the underground tunnels alive. This is so sick I have no words for it.

The roots begin to throb and pulse, their colours glowing and then flaming, writhing like snakes around the bodies of the fallen students. Then they're rippling and undulating around and into Ms Merrybourne. She half lurches forwards, her face rapturous. Around her the guards have begun chanting, their voices low and deep at first and then rising louder and louder. I want to cover my ears, but I don't dare move.

'*Aut vincere aut mori*
Aut vincere aut mori
Aut vincere aut mori'

The chanting goes on and on, and all the while, Ms Merrybourne seems to become more and more energised. Revitalised.

This is what the guard meant. This is 'the feeding'.

This is the source of Ms Merrybourne's power. The roots extract the life force from the dead students and transfer it to Ms Merrybourne, or something like that.

We turn to each other, horror, revulsion and fear written across our faces. The true meaning of the school's Latin epithet is now horrifically clear to us all.

Those who failed to conquer met their end.

Chapter 16

The horror unfolding before our eyes paralyses us. The chanting is almost hypnotic. If we're not careful, it might draw us in. I glance at the others. They're staring at the scene, open-mouthed with shock. We'll be in grave danger if we stay here any longer. If the Ravens see us then surely we'll end up inside the roots, like Will and everyone else who failed the games. I need to get us out of here. I nudge Murk beside me. She doesn't respond. I nudge her harder to get her attention, and whisper as loud as I dare. "We have to go!"

She gathers herself and nods, struggling to find words. "Right," she replies, and sends a message down the line. We have to get out of this quad.

"Which way?" I ask her. Murk's been in the school much longer than I have and I know she'll find the safest route – if there is one.

"Follow me." She starts to crawl along the hedge that hides us, and once she's close to the one behind us, she darts through an opening.

There's a row of trees with flowering bushes and raised flower beds between them. It's only several feet beyond us and we'll be well out of sight there. It leads to the outer pathway of the quad, close to the main Oak House building.

I wait, letting Belle and Jane follow Murk first, intending

to bring up the rear with Ford. As Jane passes me, I notice her pallor is deathly white, her dark eyes wide with fear. She stumbles and gasps. I know what's going through her mind – visions of her aunty having met the same fate as the other students who fell in the previous games. There's been no time to tell Jane what I discovered about her aunty winning the last prize.

"Let me get her out first, Belle," I whisper. She nods, urging me ahead.

I take a firm grip of Jane's hand. She's trembling, her hand freezing cold and clammy. "Stay close to me, Jane. And stay low," I tell her as she half rises. I pull her along as fast as I can. Murk pauses every few yards to make sure the coast is clear, and the Ravens haven't clocked us, before moving stealthily forwards again.

We dart across the pathway, and hug the side of the Oak House building, thankful for its nooks and crevices, and shuffle around the side of the building and, finally, out of the quad and behind Oak House. Jane yanks her hand out of mine and rushes towards some bushes. She ploughs into them, and then I hear sounds of vomiting. I sag back against the wall, my knees threatening to give way.

Jane emerges from the bushes, wiping her mouth. She looks so lost. I push away from the wall and go over to her. When I put my arms around her she doesn't push me away. Instead, she leans into me, sobbing quietly.

"I'm sorry, Andy," she says, as she takes a step back. She swipes at the tears rolling down her face. "Is that . . . is that what happened to my aunty? I can't bear the thought of it.

How can I tell my mum anything about what we just saw?"

"I know, but listen, Jane. When I checked out Charter House, I saw the school charter, and on the wall beside it was a list of all the previous Pentangle Prize winners. Your aunty was one of the five who won in 2000."

Jane's mouth falls open with shock. "What? Are you sure?"

"I'm positive. I saw her name."

"That means . . . I don't know," she shakes her head, baffled. "If she was a winner, then where is she?"

The question hangs in the air. I don't have an answer for her.

The others make it around the side of the building and we don't hang about. The faint tones of chanting continue, but we head away from Oak House as fast as we can. There's an archway leading into a small walled garden complete with fountains and small squares of manicured lawns interspersed with rose bushes. Most importantly, there's no one around. We find a bench and slump down on it. All we need is a quick debrief and a plan for our next move. It should be safe for a while – the guards are aware that groups and alliances have formed to get through the games, so we shouldn't stick out too much even if we are seen.

Murk can't sit still. She gets up and paces around. Her tension is palpable. "You know I'm into anime and I watch *Soul Eater* and stuff, but this is real, guys! There's no way on earth Ms Merrybourne is human. She's something else entirely."

"And the Pentangle Prize is a feeding ground for her," Belle says, anxiously chewing her lips.

Ford is looking at his trainers like they hold the answer to everything. He raises his head. "I didn't want to believe any of it. But this is seriously messed up."

We're quiet for a moment. The image of Ms Merrybourne's face in that weird enraptured state is never going to be surpassed as the worst experience of my life – and I think that goes for all of us. It's not a memory that we're ever going to be able to erase.

"We've been in the school a year and nothing like this has ever happened before. It's been normal. I just can't get my head around it." Ford's face is taut and he exhales deeply before turning to Jane. "Still want to hang around for the rest of the games?"

I can't see her face. She's beside me on the bench, but her head is resting on her drawn-up knees. "Jane?" I say softly. "Are you OK?"

She shakes her head. Finally, she raises her head. "I can't stay here." It comes out as a whisper. I place a comforting arm around her back, relieved beyond words.

"That's good to hear, Jane. You know we couldn't have gone without you," Murk says.

Jane gives a half smile. "I know you wouldn't have. So, there's something else. Andy told me about the list of the winners of the Pentangle Prize in previous years. It turns out that my aunty was one of the five winners in 2000."

Ford's dark brows draw together in a frown. "If she was a winner, then where is she?"

Jane shrugs. "I haven't got a clue. It's hopeless. I don't know what I was expecting to find, but it wasn't this." She stifles a sob.

Belle turns her warm brown eyes on Jane. "Hun, none of us were expecting anything like this."

"And it's not hopeless, Jane," I add. "We won't give up searching for your aunty. We can figure it out once we get out of here and can think straight."

Jane sits up. There's a renewed energy about her. "Listen, I've got a plan for how we can get away without being seen. Those guys we overheard last night planning to get rid of the competition said they were coming to Well House first."

"We were still at the same number of participants for today's game. So I guess they didn't show up last night?" I ask her.

Jane shakes her head. "There were Ravens patrolling outside all night."

"Probably because today's game was going to take place there," Murk points out.

"So I figure they'll try tonight," Jane says. "If I can create some kind of diversion to draw the Ravens back to Well House, that'll give us a chance to escape when they leave their posts, and save the students Adam and his gang have targeted."

"What kind of diversion?" I'm worried Jane's going to put herself in danger – not just from the Ravens, but also from Adam and his allies. I don't want her anywhere near them.

"I'll smash a few windows upstairs in Well House to alert the Ravens, then sneak out. I found a back staircase and a locked door, which I managed to pick last night, in case Adam and his crew came calling and I needed an escape. I'll get out that way and join you wherever you are."

I shake my head. "Sounds way too risky."

"Actually, we might have something here. I've been

watching the Ravens' movements," Ford says, "and they change shifts around nine o'clock. There's about ten minutes when there are very few guards in the grounds around the school. Still a few around the houses, though, so Jane could definitely grab their attention."

Jane pushes her hair away from her face. "Then it's settled."

"No! There's got to be another way," I protest. "What if you get trapped, Jane?"

"Like we're not already trapped?" she fires back.

She's got a point.

"OK, sounds like we have a plan. We can meet near the path that takes you out to the tennis courts. It's close to the back of Well House," Ford suggests.

"And that way we won't be far from you, Jane, if you run into trouble," Murk adds.

"I could sneak in earlier and hide in that hidden staircase—" I begin, but Jane cuts me off.

"The housemistress makes sure that only Well House students are in the building at night. Remember how demented she is, Andy? But thanks."

"OK, but I'll come back with you now and make sure your escape route works. It'd be good for us to know where it comes out, so we can get a view of it from where we're meeting up tonight."

"Right, let's go," Belle says. "I need a shower and some dry clothes. The water down there was evil."

Murk scrunches her face into a scowl. "Not half as evil as what was going on in the quad."

We part ways at the entrance to the walled garden. I head

back to Well House with Jane, although it's the last place I want to be. I never want to see that well again, but Jane's still in a vulnerable state and I'm concerned about this diversion plan. When we reach the Well House quad, it's deserted. There's no sign that a horrific game was played here only a few hours ago. That students died right here, beneath our feet. And we were so close to dying ourselves. Next to me, Jane is shivering, so I put my arms around her shoulders.

"Show me the back staircase and then you can get cleaned up."

"Do you mind if I get some water from the common room first? I need to swill my mouth out."

We head into the building, and in the common room, Jane grabs a glass and fills it from the water dispenser.

"The last time I was in here was after the Adder House game. That seemed bad enough, but what's happened since . . ." I shake my head, "defies belief."

"So much has happened. None of it good," Jane says between gulps of water.

"Apart from the friendships," I say, looking at her.

She tilts her head and smiles. Her eyes are moist with tears. She clears her throat. "I hope we stay alive to get to know each other better."

"We're not gonna die here, Jane," I tell her. I really want to believe that.

We head back out to the hallway.

"The hidden exit is back here." She points at a door tucked inside an alcove. "And behind is the staircase."

I try the door, but it's locked.

"It's bolted from the inside, remember? I'll create the diversion, slip down the staircase from my dorm upstairs and unbolt this door. Then I'll head out through the back door. And hopefully you'll all be waiting for me."

I open the back door and step outside. There's a clear view of the grounds and the woods beyond. Leading to the left and right are pathways, lined with hedges and trees. It's so picturesque, scenic, like it's off a postcard – which unsuspecting person wouldn't want to come to a school like this? There's nothing to reveal the horrors that lurk in every corner.

"We'll be waiting behind the hedges for you. We're going to get out, Jane," I reassure her.

"I hope you're right, Andy," she says quietly. "Thank you. For being there for me. For having my back."

She slips her arms around me, and her face rises towards mine. I go to hug her and her lips are suddenly so close to mine. I feel heat on my skin. It catches me by surprise, and she must see it on my face as she hesitates. A whirlwind of thoughts rush through my mind – fear of getting us all out alive, our vulnerability. Then there's Belle – wasn't there a connection between us? But I also can't deny that I have feelings for Jane.

I'm a mess of confusion.

In the end, her lips brush against my cheek as I turn my face.

"Sorry," she mutters, blushing. "I didn't mean that."

"I didn't . . . I wasn't, I mean. I wasn't expecting—" I mumble incoherently.

Her face has fallen. I think back to how disappointed she was that I wanted to escape; how she reacted when she first saw me and Belle together. It wasn't just because I was the first friend she'd made here or for a lack of trust of the others. How could I not have seen that she liked me that much? I'm in turmoil. I don't know if I have the same feelings for her as she has for me. And I'm afraid to say anything now in case it's the wrong thing.

She smooths back her damp hair and gives me a half smile. "I must stink like anything. I'd better get showered."

"Yeah – I mean, I do too. Stink, that is," I babble. "I'll see you at lunch."

I leave the house quickly, wondering how to deal with what just happened. With how much she likes me. And . . . do I like her in the same way?

Chapter 17

I arrive in the dining hall alone, wishing I'd arranged to meet one of the others first. The atmosphere is chilly and the high ceilings and stone walls make me shiver. Earlier, I stood under the shower on the hottest setting I could stand until I was as wrinkled as an old prune, but it still didn't warm me up. The icy, dank water of the underground tunnels has seeped into my bones.

Muted voices echo around me. In no way does the dining hall resemble the excited buzz of the first day of induction when there were a hundred students in here, all talking and chatting and happy and eager.

Now there are only twenty of us – and most of them are scowling at me.

Two of the LNS are already sitting at our table at the back of the room, so I head over to them, ignoring the surly looks I get from the other students huddled in their alliances. Piers and his gang are at one table. Amy is with them, which makes me sad. She's the one who thought the Ravens were all for show – all part of the test. Even she can't have imagined how deadly real these games would become. Adam and his plotters are parked at another table. Everyone is a plotter now though, aren't they? Everyone poses a threat.

We've been culled, like animals, and the culling isn't

over yet. Only five students will remain alive at the end of the final game. Fifteen of us won't survive.

Jane and Murk are yet to arrive, so I'm not last. I stride past the tables towards Belle and Ford. They're talking, their chairs pulled close and their heads almost touching. I slow my pace, and feel a twinge of jealousy at seeing them together. But, putting my bruised feelings aside, a part of me thinks maybe it's a good thing for them that they've rediscovered something. Maybe they're meant to be together, and these awful games have shown them that.

It would be one positive to come out of the chaos we're submerged in. It's thrown me and Jane closer together too. I admire her so much for risking her life to uncover the truth about her aunty. She's got so much strength, but I've seen her vulnerability too. What she tried to undertake on her own was way too much for one person to handle.

The fight for survival has brought all of us together. If we get through this, it will always be a part of our lives and no one else could possibly understand the trauma of it, or what it took from us. My parents will have to take out a second mortgage to pay for the therapy I'm going to need!

It's not a laughing matter, I'm well aware of that. These games must be making me hysterical. That's what this school has done to me. There's no way that a guaranteed place at an elite uni is something worth paying this price for. I can still follow my dream of going to uni and being a surgeon. If I live.

Belle gives me a weak smile as I approach the table. I still remember her cute smile, complete with dimples, when

I caught her on camera on that first day. I want to rewind to that first day again and for everything to be normal, for this school to be normal, to have a proper induction week and lessons and homework and all that boring stuff. Yes, even the boring stuff! Anything but this. I push away thoughts of home and of Mum and Dad and being a normal kid as I sit down with Belle and Ford. "Hey. It's frosty in here, isn't it? Or is it just me?"

"Everyone's got their gang – five in each," Ford says, pointing the chicken drumstick he's gnawing on at me. That boy has the appetite of a tiger. "They figure it's the only way to win."

"And they're not wrong," Murk says, slipping into the chair beside me. "It's a dangerous time to be alive. We need to totally watch our backs now. Those guys would take us out without the slightest hesitation."

Jane arrives and takes the chair next to Ford. "Hey," she says.

Her eyes flick past me quickly. I really don't want there to be any awkwardness between us, but I'm not sure how to fix it.

"Everything cool with the plan for later?" Ford asks her.

She nods. "Yeah."

"Jane's scouted out a good escape route. But I'd be happier if I was in the house with her to help out in case—"

"I'll be fine, Andy," Jane jumps in. "No sense in risking two of us being caught at Well House."

"Are you sure?" Belle has dropped her voice to a whisper. "If it's too dangerous, we can think up something else."

"I'm pretty decent at sneaking around, so I can always get

to your house earlier and then do the smash and run with you," Murk offers.

"Seriously, I can handle it," Jane replies. "Worry about yourselves."

"We can position ourselves with a decent view of the door Jane's planning on escaping through, so if she gets into trouble then we're not far from her," I add.

I'm trying, but Jane's barely spared me a glance, which makes me feel guilty – and more than a bit regretful about the way I handled the situation earlier. Her hand is trembling as she takes a sip of water. She's probably still rattled from everything that's happened today. We all are, but for her it's personal because of the mystery of what's happened to her aunty. It begs the question: what happens to the winners?

If by some miracle the LNS win the games, what will happen to us?

***

Time drags its feet until it is almost nine o'clock. My pulse is racing and there's little I can do to stop it. It's already dark as I head out of Charter House. This time I have to make doubly sure that I'm not followed. I circle around the quad, hugging the shadows and then stop and put my foot up on a bench, pretending to do up my laces. I glance around. It's quiet with not a soul in sight, so I make for the path running along the side of Charter House, which leads to the back of the building.

I see no one and, hopefully, no one sees me. On the other side of the building an expanse of gardens opens up. If I follow the path, it'll lead me past the back of Oak House and then to the meeting point, which is close to Well House. Close to Jane.

I pop my headphones in, but I don't play any music. It's got to look as though I'm destressing with an evening walk, which I have never done in my life before. But if there was ever a moment when I needed to destress, it'd be right now. I bob my head side to side to the pretend music, my hands clenched tight in the pockets of my hoodie, and my heart pumping a thousand times a second.

Idly, I cross the lawn and sit on the grass. I pluck at blades of grass as I take in the layout of the back of the school. I have a good view of the backs of the buildings and the paths running around them. There's still no one around, so I get to my feet and head for the meeting point. I walk past it without breaking a stride. Someone whistles softly, twice. That's the signal it's clear. I walk swiftly around the back of the hedge and duck down. Belle, Murk and Ford are all here.

"So far so good," Ford says. He's pressed against the hedge. "We've got a clear view of the back of Well House from here."

"There's still a couple of minutes before nine," Belle says.

"And then all hell will break loose." Murk grins. "We'll either make it, or we'll be demon dinner." Ford turns around and glares at Murk. She raises her hands in apology. "Just trying to introduce some levity."

"It's time to get serious, Murk," Ford says. "And we've got to figure out another meeting place if we somehow get split up in the woods."

"We're not going to get split up," Belle says.

"In case, though. It could happen," Ford insists.

“We should try to stick together as much as poss. Otherwise, how will we know to help someone if they’re in trouble?” I ask.

Ford shrugs and goes back to watching through the hedge. He turns back and raises his finger to his lips. We hunker down further and peer through the hedge. Three Ravens are at the far end of the back of Well House. It looks as though they’re doing their rounds before the change of shift. The timing is out, though – shouldn’t they have done the outer path already?

How will Jane know to wait a bit longer before smashing the glass? I glance at my watch. Ten seconds left before it hits nine. The guards draw alongside us and one of them flashes his torch at the hedges. None of us breathe. He moves on with the others. They’re heading for the path that will take them around the front of Well House. *Please wait another few seconds, Jane! Wait for the guards to round the corner.* But she can’t see them and our phones don’t work, so there’s no way we can get a message to her.

It's too late. My watch hits nine on the dot, and right on cue, the sound of smashing glass shatters the quiet of the night. Jane has made her move.

One of the guards moves off to the front of Well House to investigate the noise, but the other two are still standing there. The faceless, robed figures are talking to each other. I strain my ears but they’re too far away for me to catch a single word. They seem to have reached a decision though. One of them moves towards the back exit of Well House, while the other follows the path around to the front.

Another glass smashes from inside the building. What's Jane doing? Does she sense it's not going according to plan? That the guards haven't been drawn away to check what's going on?

We look at each other, caught in indecision. We can't help Jane. And there's no way she can escape through the back of the house with the Raven standing there. She'll be caught. Unless she can slip away later. But what if she can't?

Should we help ourselves and get away while we can?

Chapter 18

There's a slim opening, a chance to get away, and I can tell from his expression, and the way he's just gestured towards the woods with his thumb, that Ford thinks we should take it and run while we can.

I shake my head angrily. "We can't go without her."

"All our lives are at stake," Ford says. "She was the only one who insisted she wanted to stay."

"Yeah, but she changed her mind," I remind him. "And it's only because of her that we have this chance to escape."

"OK, you stay, but we have to take this opportunity to get out of here. We'll wait in the shed near the tennis courts and if you're not there in twenty minutes, we'll head into the woods."

"Fine." I'm so angry with Ford, but he's right, I guess. No sense in us all dying here.

"I'll stay with Andy," Murk says.

"I can handle it alone, Murk. You should get away with the others, and get help," I tell her. "Please."

Murk pauses, torn. "No way am I leaving my mates behind."

"Jane would want you to go and get help! Please, Murk," I say fiercely.

She opens her mouth, another protest forming, but in the end she throws up her hands and nods.

They hunker down on their hands and knees and scuttle away, then pause as the noise level from Well House goes up decibels. The students in there are panicking, yelling and shouting at each other. A cloaked guard is leaning out of one of the upstairs windows and calling for the Raven at the back exit. He hurries into the building.

"We need to move. Now! If we wait any longer, the guards are likely to spot us," Belle urges. "That means you too, Andy. It'll give Jane a chance to get away."

But will it? What if she runs into trouble and needs help?

"Stick to the plan, Andy!" Ford snaps.

I know it's logical and it makes sense, but I can't bring myself to move. I made Jane a promise.

The others have already moved off, but my feet refuse to follow them. I've made my decision: I'm staying. My eyes flick back and forth between watching their progress, and watching Well House, desperate for a sign of Jane. The others are almost at the edge of the grounds and then they disappear from sight.

It's just me now.

Come on, Jane. Where are you? I won't leave here without you.

I hear more shouting from the house, but I can't tell where it's coming from. Figures flit across the windows at the back of the house. I'm so close to leaving my hiding place and going to find Jane when I see her.

She's made it to the back door of Well House. She's glancing around wildly, looking for us. I half stand so she can see me beckoning her. "This way!" I yell.

And then she's flying across the path towards me as fast

as she can. Relief floods through me. We might actually make it; we might get out of this place alive.

I throw my arms around her as she reaches me, clutching her close for a moment. She clings tightly, too, and it feels right with us again. Then we both take off, racing across the grounds.

Barely a few strides in, we hear shouts.

"Get them!" someone screams.

I glance back to see a Raven at one of the windows, pointing at us. We've been spotted.

We're almost at the edge of the woods, but behind us two Ravens are giving chase, their feet pounding across the ground, their black cloaks billowing behind them.

"Run faster!" I cry.

We plough into the woods. The plan of getting out of the school grounds past the tennis courts is forgotten. We're running for our lives, our feet crunching across autumn leaves, trampling through bracken and twigs, making more than enough racket to raise the dead, and definitely enough for our pursuers to hear.

We're so far behind the others I have no idea which direction they went. I grab Jane's arm and we veer off to the right where the trees are denser and will give us extra cover. We duck under branches and dodge trees and thickets. The ground beneath our feet is shrouded in darkness like the rest of the woods, but it's too risky to switch on my phone torch. A quick glance behind tells me we have to run faster. The lights of the guards' torches are bobbing in and out of the trees as they pursue us.

"Stop!" one of them yells. "There's no escape."

"You're in so much trouble!" the other calls out.

They're not going to give up until they've caught us. I just hope there's a way out of here through the woods, because if there isn't . . . we definitely will be in so much trouble. I can almost hear Ms Merrybourne's cackling laughter as she says that word that strikes dread into our hearts.

'*Elimination*'.

No one is going to eliminate me. I'm not going to let them. And I'm sure the guards didn't see how many of us were making a break for freedom, so it's just possible they only saw me and Jane, which will give Murk, Belle and Ford a chance to get away.

But I'm not ready to give up yet. I studied the layout of the school and the grounds – we all did – as preparation for this escape, but in the panic of the moment and the disorientation of the dark woods, it's gone right out of my head. I'm pretty sure Merrybourne village lies east of the school. Ford's plan was to head towards the tennis courts and then circle back southeast to the village, making it harder for anyone who might be tracking us.

But I've lost my bearings and I've got no idea which way is east.

"Are we headed the right way?" I pant.

Jane's breathing is laboured. She stops and leans on a tree, trying to catch her breath. "I don't know. I'm sorry, I've no idea where we are."

There's a compass app on my phone, but will it work without reception? I pull out my phone and stab at the app.

"What are you doing?" Jane's gasps out.

"Checking the compass. That way is east." I point. "Let's go."

I lead the way, creeping as softly but as swiftly as I can through the undergrowth in the hope that we can lose the guards. If they don't hear us charging through the woods, they won't know which direction we've gone in. I'm no Aragorn, though, and I have no Ranger skills that make me light-footed or able to see in the dark, but adrenaline is coursing through me and my senses are heightened. The Ravens' voices float through the woods. They're still behind us, but they're not as fast as us.

A building looms up in front of us. Stone walls, arched windows, with a bell-tower at one end. It's an ancient church or a chapel. One of the windows is broken and the walls are covered in moss and grime. I stop for a second to think. The Ravens will expect us to head straight for the village, not take refuge in an old chapel.

"Come on," I whisper to Jane. "We'll hide in here and catch our breath."

We creep around to the front of the chapel and push open the door. It groans loudly on its rusty hinges, and we both wince. I don't risk opening the door any wider. We slide through the gap and enter the chapel. It's dark and musty and damp. I take a chance and flick on my phone torch, pointing it low. There are pews on either side of the aisle, with an altar at the far end of the chapel. I flick the torch off and head down the aisle. We've only gone halfway when we spot a light through the windows moving alongside the chapel, heading around to the front of the building.

My heart starts thumping overtime. "Quick!"

Jane doesn't need telling twice. We slip down the aisle and slide in behind the altar. Jane clamps her hand over her mouth just as I realise how dusty the altar is. *Please don't sneeze now, Jane*, I pray.

The creaking of the chapel door opening wide splits the air. I hold my breath. Light floods the space. The Raven has walked in. He must be checking down each side of the pews.

"I know you're here. Come on out."

I recognise his voice, but where from?

"Don't make me have to come and drag you out. Make it easy on yourselves," he says. "There's no escape from Merrybourne."

I definitely know that voice, but how's that possible? I hardly know any of the teachers. I must have heard the Raven's voice before, on the way to one of the games, maybe. This isn't the best hiding place, either. When he makes it down the aisle the first place he'll check is behind the altar.

We're trapped.

I could punch myself for not thinking it through. It was a stupid plan, the worst, and now we're going to get caught and it's my fault. Jane tugs at my arm and I turn to look at her. She points at a door tucked away behind us. Can we make it across to it without being seen? We have to try – it's our only hope. We shuffle slowly across to it, hoping the guard's still scouting down each pew.

I reach the door first and raise my hand to open it just as the Raven's torchlight swings our way.

"Hey! Stop right there!" the Raven yells.

I yank the door open. *Please let it not be a store cupboard.*

It's not. There's a wooden staircase. It must go up to the bell tower. I lead the way. We race up, the ancient staircase creaking and cracking under our feet, but the wood is holding. The Raven has reached the bottom of the stairs. He's shouting and cursing as he follows us.

And then Jane screams.

I turn back to see the Raven has got hold of her foot. She's several steps behind me, but he's already trying to drag her back down. She's trying to lever herself up the stairs away from him, but he's too strong.

As I rush back to help her, I visualise Jane lashing out with her free foot and booting him in the face before scrambling away. The guard has nothing to cling to and falls backwards down the stairs.

As though Jane can hear my thoughts, she does exactly that.

I see her foot connecting with the Raven's face, still concealed under his hood. He yelps with surprise, not expecting Jane to attack him. Then it's like someone has hit the slo-mo button. The Raven rocks backwards, his arms flapping in the air as he tries to grab hold of Jane. But she scurries up a few steps. He tries to grab at the wall, but the force he put into holding on to Jane has worked against him and now that same force propels him backwards. The momentum gathers once he's released Jane's foot, and he's flailing, tipping backwards, before toppling all the way down the stairs. The stone floor looms up to meet his head and there's a horrible, gut-wrenching crack as the two connect.

Jane cries out. I'm frozen in place, shocked. We might have just killed a man. There's no way he could have survived that fall. The Raven is dead.

And it happened exactly the way I saw it in my mind's eye.

The whole sequence played out as I willed it to, every single move. I know it must be a coincidence.

Right?

Chapter 19

I break my inertia and scramble down the steps to Jane. Her chest is heaving as she gasps for air. Her eyes are wild. I know the signs – she's in the midst of a panic attack. Vik has them too, so my parents told me what to do if it happens when they're not around.

I kneel on the step in front of her, careful to give her space. "It's OK, Jane. Breathe, slowly. Come on, in slowly and then out slowly," I say soothingly. "Will it help if I hold you?"

She nods and I sit on the step beside her, my arm loosely draped around her shoulders. Her body is trembling, but gradually her rapid breathing slows.

"What happened, Andy?" she asks, her voice barely above a whisper. "I don't understand."

I don't fully understand either. It's like I foresaw the Raven's end. Or willed it to happen. But how can that possibly be true?

"He was trying to grab you and you kicked him," I say. "He fell and smacked his head."

"But I couldn't shake his hold. He had too tight a grip on my foot. I'm not that strong, Andy, and he's twice the size of me."

"Adrenaline and the fear of being caught must have given you that extra strength," I tell her, hoping that explanation will be enough to stall her doubts.

She's shaking her head. "No, no, it felt weird. Like I wasn't in control of myself. It wasn't me who lashed out like that."

"What do you mean? No one else is here. Listen, Jane, nothing about this whole thing is normal and it's changed us. We're on high alert every second of the day, surrounded by people who want to kill us, so we're constantly trying to protect ourselves. We're in self-defence mode. And that's what you were doing – acting in self-defence."

"I know it sounds crazy, but I didn't do it," she insists. "I just . . . can't explain it."

I don't know what to tell her. I'm so afraid of what the truth could be that I can barely bring myself to think about it. *Did I will this person's death?*

Jane's head sinks into her hands. "Will this nightmare never end?"

I crouch on the step below so that I'm at her eye level. "It will," I say, with all the confidence I can muster. "Come on, let's get going."

Jane cringes as she steps past the inert body of the guard towards the doorway back into the chapel.

I hesitate as I go past the Raven. Something is niggling at me.

I'm about to join Jane, but still I hesitate. Did I catch sight of a glint of gold?

"Let's get out of here, Andy," Jane says, anxious to put some distance between her and the dead Raven. I start to follow, but I'm drawn back to the Raven. "What's wrong?" she asks.

The Raven's mouth is slightly ajar and there's the glint of gold again. "I'm not sure." I bend down and pull his hood back for a better look at his face. I lurch away from him, breathing hard.

I recognise the Raven.

Jane shakes my arm. "Andy? What is it?"

"It's – it's the bus driver, the one who dropped me off at the school a few days ago. What was it he said to me? Oh, yes. 'Good luck to you', and then he'd cackled to himself. He was in on it the whole time."

Jane's mouth forms an O. "And I killed him."

"No. He died from hitting his head on the stone floor, which you couldn't have predicted."

"Andy—" she begins, but I cut her short.

"It doesn't matter – it was us or him. He took us to the school, knowing all along what was going to happen." I shake my head. "Let's go. He's not the only Raven searching for us."

I take Jane's arm and we hurry through the chapel together.

Outside, the moon has come up and casts a soft glow on the small clearing. The chapel is in the middle of the woods, surrounded by the silhouettes of shadowy trees. I use the compass app to work out which direction the village lies. I'm still dithering when we hear voices.

More Ravens.

This time I'm not going to get us trapped again. We dive into a nearby thicket, my sweatshirt snagging on brambles as we crouch down, our faces close to the earthy mustiness of the damp soil. I hope they pass by us quickly, but they're bound to check inside the chapel first, and when they do, they'll find the dead Raven and raise the alarm. I should have got us deeper into the woods before checking directions. My heart is thudding loudly. Jane reaches for my hand. We hold on to each other, and wait.

"I've heard this has only ever happened a couple of times before," a woman's voice says.

"I wouldn't know, this is my first time," a male voice replies.

"There was one runaway in 2000. Looks as though there are at least a couple of kids on the loose tonight, maybe more."

"So this is serious, I guess," the male Raven says.

"Of course it is, you idiot! This is going to cause us major problems," the female Raven snaps.

The man grunts. "No need to shout. I don't want to be traipsing around the woods at night either. The kids won't escape. They were doomed the minute they set foot on school grounds. We'll catch them – it's only a matter of time – and then they'll be in trouble."

"Don't be so naïve. We're the ones on duty tonight, so we're the ones who'll be punished. Trust me. You don't want to incur the demon's wrath."

The demon's wrath? What the actual hell!

Jane clutches my arm and we turn to look at each other, both of us struggling to absorb what we've just heard. We draw closer together.

"She's a demon?" Jane hisses under her breath.

I raise my finger to my lips. The Ravens are still talking.

The man's tone changes. "Then we'd better find them fast."

"I've called in back-up. We absolutely can't let them escape the woods."

"Let's check out the chapel before we go any further.

It's as good a hiding place as any. We might find a couple of them lurking in here."

The Ravens' voices go quiet as they push the creaky chapel door open wide and disappear inside.

The coast is clear, but it won't be for long. They'll find the body and then all hell will break loose. I have to completely ignore what the Ravens said about the demon because it's too frightening to even contemplate. And fear will paralyse us. We need to get far, far away from here.

I've already checked on my compass app and got my bearings. Merrybourne village is still east of our position. Staying low, we scramble through the thicket and the undergrowth. Taking a second to make sure we're not being watched, we scour the woods for any other torchlights – any sign of more Ravens coming to join the search. It's clear for now.

Hand in hand, we race through the woods towards Merrybourne village – and, hopefully, the rest of the Lost Name Society.

Chapter 20

I'm running on autopilot, barely able to focus. There are so many thoughts and questions racing around my head. *A demon.* We're fighting a demon! And that's not all. Can I really influence other people's behaviour? Because that's what seems to have happened in the chapel. Did I really make Jane kill the Raven?

How?

I stumble over a protruding tree root as I realise that I've only witnessed one other person wield control over others like that . . . Ms Merrybourne.

"You OK?" Jane checks.

I nod, feeling anything but OK. My mind is racing faster than my feet. I need to think about this logically – not easy to do when you're on the run.

The only thing I can think of is that the pages I ripped out of the charter must have played a part in this. They're significant. I know the charter is magical in some way – I saw those threads knit themselves together with my own eyes. Then later, I passed the pages I'd taken from the charter around to the LNS and they wrote their *real* names on them and gave them back to me. So am I somehow able to make the Lost Namers do what I want them to do? I must have the same powers of control as the demon possesses over the rest of the students. My mind is reeling. I don't want that kind of power. I don't want to be able to control my friends' actions. I don't want any of this!

A stab of guilt wracks through me. *I made Jane kill the guard.*

There's no way I could ever tell her about this because she'll never forgive me. I'll lose her friendship, and . . . it means so much to me. I can't tell any of the others either. They'll never trust me again.

"Which way now?" Jane whispers.

We've reached the edge of the woods. The village lies before us. A hundred yards up the road, away from the village, I spy a sign for Merrybourne.

WELCOME TO MERRYBOURNE
TWINNED WITH Chateau-le-Satin

The meeting point.

Keeping within a couple of feet inside the line of trees along the road, we make for the sign, hoping against hope the others have made it here safely. We reach the sign, but no one's here. Jane and I look at each other. I shrug. "We wait," I whisper. We move back, so we're not visible from the road. An owl hoots in the dark silence. We hear another sound: shuffling. It's coming from further inside the woods.

"Andy! Jane!"

It's Ford's voice. We peer into the thicket of trees. It's pitch black and we can't see a thing.

"Over here." Murk's face appears briefly before she ducks down again.

We move through the dense tangle of trees towards her,

and as soon as we reach her she throws her arms around us, followed by Belle and Ford. It's so emotional I feel myself tearing up, and notice the others are too. We're all stunned that we actually made it, actually got away from the hellhole that is Merrybourne School.

I just hope that Merrybourne village is normal and that we can find help. Because we desperately need it.

"Everyone OK?" I ask them. "Anyone follow you?"

"We lost them before we headed this way. Murk laid a false trail for them. It should hold them off for a while," Ford says. He sounds proud of Murk.

"What about you guys?" Belle asks. She touches Jane's arm. "Hey, are you OK?"

Jane has barely spoken a word. Her eyes are glazed as she mumbles, "Yes," to Belle, and pulls away.

"What's happened?" Ford asks, looking between me and Jane. He glances over our shoulders. "Are you sure you lost them?"

"Of course we lost them. We took care," I snap. I can't help the anger creeping into my voice.

"Something's wrong," he insists.

"Take a look around, Ford. Everything's wrong!" I'm seething at Ford and all his questions. He was the one who wanted us to split up in the first place, and then he wanted to abandon Jane. "We've got to get help as fast as possible – that's all that matters now."

"Yeah, but—" Ford begins.

"Drop it, Ford," Murk cuts in. "In case you've forgotten, we've got Ravens on our tail. They won't think we've made it to the village yet, so let's go."

We turn towards the village, using the trees as cover, until we run out of trees and have to take to the open paths. The village is dimly lit with widely-spaced streetlamps. Everything is neat and tidy: the gardens have that freshly mown look, the houses are adorned with hanging baskets bursting with flowers, and there's not a single item of litter on the ground. It's a picturesque village – I remember it from when I was waiting for the bus outside the train station. On my first day. At the time, it felt nice, and it felt normal, safe. It was daytime then. At night it doesn't feel like any of those things. There's a creepy edge to the village. There are no lights on in any of the houses. There is no one taking their dog for a late walk, no teenagers hanging around, no couples walking back from a meal out at the local pub.

It's deathly silent.

We try to soften our footfalls as we run. I glance at the windows of the houses, shrouded in darkness, and a shiver tingles down my spine. I hope no one is watching us from behind their curtains. We couldn't look more suspicious racing through the village in our school tracksuits, with fear etched on our faces. "How far is the police station?" I ask.

Belle grimaces. "I'm not sure, but it might be at the other end of the village. I've never noticed it when I've been down here." Her mouth quirks. "Never needed to know before."

"None of us come down here much, if we can help it," Murk adds in a low voice.

The village is bigger than I first thought. The main road seems to run the length of it, so we continue, trying to make as little noise as possible.

"Stop!" Ford suddenly hisses, skidding to a halt.

An old man has turned out of a side road directly in front of us. He's the first person we've encountered since arriving in the village.

He stops and stares at us like we're apparitions. His mouth falls open and his eyes widen. Then he glances around furtively before looking more closely at us.

"You're from the school?" He points at the logos on our tracksuits. "How the hell did you get out? What are you doing here?"

He must know what's going on at Merrybourne!

Belle answers first. "Running away." She clasps her hands, pleading. "Please, will you help us?"

"You're not safe here. You must get away! Quickly!"

"We know," Ford says. "Don't worry, no one followed us." Ford shoots me a look.

"Then go!" the old man barks. "It's not safe!"

"We need to get help for the other kids at the school," I insist.

"No! You must go now!"

"Listen, mate," Ford begins, getting impatient.

I interrupt him. "It's not safe for us in the village, is that what you mean?" I ask the old guy more gently. He seems completely thrown by our presence, and the way he'd asked: 'How the hell did you get out?' – is chilling.

The old man leans in. "This place is even more dangerous than the school." His eyes are constantly scanning the streets and the houses around us. "You must leave the village at once.

Get away, as far away as possible."

"Just tell us where the police station is and we'll go," Ford persists.

"No, no, no. Do not go there. They won't help you," the old man says, horrified.

Ford throws up his hands in exasperation. "Of course they will. It's their job, isn't it? The students are in danger."

The old man gets right up close in Ford's face. "And they'll be in even more danger if you go to the police."

Jane pulls Ford away from the old man. "We can't trust the police to help us."

We all know the story of how little the police did when Jane's aunty went missing. This is different though. Surely the police would have to listen to us. Right?

"We've got nowhere else to go," Belle pleads with the man again. "Please, can you help us?"

The old man curses and takes an age to come to a decision. "All right, come with me. No one else is trustworthy in the village."

Is this true? Bar banging on doors and waking up half the village, or taking our chances at the police station, what other choice do we have?

"I'd rather take our chances with going to the police than following him," Ford says, backing away.

"Listen, Ford!" Jane says urgently. "The police won't help us! I'm not going anywhere near them."

"I'm with Jane on this," Murk adds. "It's a horrible village and the police will simply march us straight back to school. Andy, what do you think?"

This man could be leading us to the Ravens for all we know, but he seems genuinely worried for us. Appearances can be deceptive, though, as we've learnt from our very own uber-glamorous Ms Merrybourne. I haven't yet told the others about the conversation me and Jane overheard about '*the demon*'.

And as though he's heard my thoughts, the old man says, "I beg you not to go to the police station." He drops his voice lower. "The influence of the demon is far-reaching. It's corrupted the village at every level – and that includes the police."

"Whoa!" Murk's hands fly to her head. "For real? We're dealing with a demon?"

"You know of whom I speak," the old man says. "It's true. That's why you cannot be seen in the village. Everyone is in league with that horror from hell!"

Dread fills each and every one of us.

He's confirmed what the two Ravens in the woods said, but it's still shocking. When I find my voice, I say, "He's telling the truth about the demon." I quickly tell them what Jane and I overheard.

"Hush, boy." The old man is getting more and more agitated. "You must come with me now! Or run for your lives!"

We waste no more time arguing and follow him. The old man's ankle-length brown coat flaps behind him as he strides down the main road, but within a few metres he takes a sharp right down a small side street, and then down another street, well away from the main road. At the end of the lane is a pretty little cottage, honey-stoned with black timber beams. It looks like it's at least 300-400 years old.

Silence hangs like a heavy mantle over the village, so it's a relief when he ushers us through the door and into the living room. Before he shuts the door, he checks up and down the lane, making sure we haven't been seen entering the cottage.

"Let's hope no one's been watching," he says, leading us into the living room. "My name is Fred Simmonds, and I have no idea how you managed to escape the school, but I will do all that I can to help you."

I'm surprised. I know that name – or the Simmonds part of it at least. It can't be that common a name in a village. "Are you any relation to the mayor? To Jim Simmonds?"

Fred's eyes darken. "Yes. He's my brother," he replies. "And he, too, cannot be trusted."

Chapter 21

I don't understand it. Why is the whole village under the thrall of a demon? What is it that connects this place to the school? Obviously it shares the same name, and our headmistress has the same title. Is it all to do with names? Is that the key? There've got to be some answers that Fred can give us.

"Why do consecutive headteachers take the same name as the village? And why is the village following orders from the demon at the school? And the police too?"

"I'll do my best to help you escape. Lie low here until we come up with a plan to smuggle you out of the village. That's all I can do for you," Fred says, not answering any of my questions.

"But we need to know more. It doesn't make sense!" Ford exclaims in frustration. "Sorry, but somehow we've got to get help, and without more knowledge how can we explain what's going on? No one's going to believe us."

"Please, Fred. You've helped us so far and we really appreciate it. Can you tell us anything else?"

But even Belle's charm isn't working on him. Fred's pacing the room, wearing holes into his shoes. "Look, kids, as much as I'd like to do more, I can't. Don't ask more of me. I've said too much already."

"They'll kill us. It'll be on your conscience for ever,"

Jane says quietly. "You *must* tell us what's going on."

Something in her tone makes Fred stop pacing. He crumples into an armchair. "Whatever I tell you will never be believed by anyone outside of this village. And inside this village – no one will care."

"We have a right to know. Our lives are at stake," Jane persists. "They want us dead."

Long seconds pass. Fred wraps his arms around himself as though he's cold. "Grab a seat," he says finally, in a resigned tone. "It's a long story. It starts way back in the seventeenth century, during the Black Death. Perhaps you've studied it at school."

We nod and take a seat as he suggests. What could the Black Death possibly have to do with what's going on at the school?

"It was a terrible time – particularly if you were in London," Fred continues. "If someone had the plague, they were boarded up in their homes with the rest of their family. A guard was stationed outside to ensure no one left the house. Inevitably, the whole family contracted the disease and died. At night, the wagons took away the dead. Huge pits were filled with dead bodies.

"The symptoms were horrific. People coughed up blood, they were feverish and delirious. They suffered swellings across their body and terrible cramps. Some people kept it quiet if a family member showed symptoms. They didn't want to be locked up in their homes with a diseased person, and risk falling sick themselves. They'd carry on as normal, and so the plague spread. Right across London. The Royal

Court decamped to Oxford. The wealthy ran away to their country estates. The poor had nowhere to go. The streets gradually emptied as the plague spread like wildfire across the capital, and thousands upon thousands of people died. Cats and dogs were put down in the fear that they might be carriers of the disease. Turned out it was rats, but no one knew that then."

Fred rubs his eyes and takes a deep breath. "It was when there were signs that the plague had begun to spread outside the old walls of London that folk here became concerned. What if it reached the village? What if a plague carrier brought it here unknowingly? There were no symptoms for the first couple of days of contracting the disease, so you wouldn't know you had it, but you could spread it far and wide. It would take just one person to bring the plague here and it would spell the demise of our village. Merrybourne's founders prayed for the health and prosperity of the villagers, prayed that the plague would not reach our village. They prayed so good and so hard that their prayers were answered."

We glance at each other. All of us remember when the school was first founded, and when the first games were played.

Fred shakes his head sorrowfully. "But not in a way that they expected." He pauses for a moment. "Their prayers were answered by a demon of discord. The demon was very clever. It offered a guarantee of survival and prosperity. Who could refuse such a generous offer? Not our founders, that is for certain. They accepted the demon's condition." Fred falls silent.

"What was the condition?" I prompt. "Fred?"

We see the anguish in his eyes. "That the founders sacrifice new souls every quarter century. The demon's charter was signed by each and every one of Merrybourne's leaders. They reasoned that sacrificing souls every twenty-five years was a fair price for prosperity and power. Look at our village." Fred raises his arms. "Is it not beautiful? We want for nothing here. We are healthy and wealthy. What more could you want?" Fred's voice drops. "What our esteemed founders did not realise was that by signing the charter, they were giving consent to the demon to influence and amplify their every thought and action – including every dark thought, every dark action. The demon feeds on humans' discontent and negative energy."

We sit in stunned silence, trying to make sense of what Fred's telling us. He's talked about the village, not the school, and I wonder how they are linked.

"So that's the short history of Merrybourne village and the Black Death. Ever since the founders signed that charter centuries ago, there's been strict control over who lives here. It's why most families here can be traced back generations. But every newcomer *must* sign to live here . . ." Fred's voice sounds strained with the weight of his words, and he clears his throat. "The demon masquerades as your headmistress and is able to influence not only the students who've signed up for the Pentangle Prize but every resident in the village – with their written consent, whether that consent is given knowingly or unknowingly. The demon can also harness the energy of animals and objects."

"The Oak Tree," Belle says with a shudder.

"The well and the water in it," Jane says.

"The adders' nest," I add. "So why are you helping us, Fred? How *can* you help? Aren't you under the demon's influence too – like all the other villagers?"

"*Every* villager must sign the charter when they come of age, but, unlike my dear brother Jim, I have always hated what happens here. It's not right. I want nothing more than to leave this place, health and wealth be damned! But it's more than that. If I, or anyone else, ignore the condition of the original charter, the demon will take *our* souls. Our spirits will never find peace. So I cannot leave the village. I'm tied to it, and, yes, my mind can be influenced by the demon." Fred taps his nose and whispers, "I have a secret. I keep a journal of my true thoughts, so that I always remember the truth of this place. When I come out of a trance and forget what is real, I need only to read my journal."

"And the school? How does the school come into it?" Murk asks.

"It's a terrible thing to admit, but on some level I do understand why the founders wanted to protect the village from the plague that doomed so many people. The first soul sacrificed to the demon was Captain Merrybourne – immortalised by your school statue. He was the first headmaster of the school. Since 1675, the sacrifice has been students at the school. The ones who play the Pentangle Prize Championship."

"So by founding the school, the villagers have knowingly avoided sacrificing themselves. It's a loophole. Instead, they sacrifice the souls of boarders from Merrybourne School?"

Belle is aghast.

"Correct. Everyone's too afraid for their lives to break the charter, and the demon gets the best sacrifices from a large pool of students at the school," Fred gravely confirms. "The villagers live on peacefully and benefit from the deal struck with the demon centuries ago."

Jane leans forwards, an intent expression on her face. "What becomes of the winners of the games?"

Fred opens his mouth to answer just as a resounding crash splits the air. It sounds as though the cottage door has been smashed off its hinges. "Run!" he cries.

We leap to our feet, but it's too late. Hooded Ravens rush in and grab hold of us. Two pin Fred to his chair. I'm pinned to the floor with my arms yanked back and held tight by another Raven.

We hear slow steady footsteps tapping across the wooden floor of the hallway. My heart plummets. I know those footsteps can only belong to one person.

"Well, well, well," Ms Merrybourne says, clapping her hands delightedly. "What do we have here? I see you were having a party and neglected to invite me. How rude of you. We decided to gatecrash it, or rather," she glances back towards the smashed door in the hallway, "door-crash it." She laughs, but her laughter has not one iota of warmth to it.

"You can't keep us against our will," Ford yells.

"We've called for help," I say urgently. "You should let us go before they get here."

"Nice try, my dears, but no one is coming to your aid.

There is no escape. Such a pity it had to be you five. I had high hopes for you. Oh well." She glowers at us, and we shrink back.

Ms Merrybourne approaches Fred. "Fred, you have been misbehaving. Your brother will be so disappointed in you. You always were the black sheep of the family. I want you to go upstairs now." Fred nods obediently and shuffles to his feet. "You know what you need to do," she adds cryptically.

He stumbles to the hallway without looking at us, his face blank, his eyes unfocused. We hear his tread on the stairs as he climbs upstairs.

"Let them sit," Ms Merrybourne instructs the Ravens. She goes towards the window and pulls the drapes open. "A fine night for it," she remarks.

What is she talking about? Our failed escape? Is she going to kill us here?

I can hear Belle sobbing, but I can't reach her to comfort her. Jane's gone into shut-down again. I twist around and catch sight of Murk. She's still struggling to break loose, and it takes two Ravens to keep hold of her. Before long, she sees how fruitless it is and stops. The room descends into silence. We're waiting for whatever is going to come next. *Why didn't we leave Merrybourne and run to the next village, the next town? Why did we head for this damned village?* But it's too late for those kinds of thoughts.

The creaking of the floorboards upstairs breaks the silence. What is Fred doing? It sounds like he's opening a window in the room right above the living room. Our attention snaps towards the living room window as something goes flying past. It pulls back up and hangs right in front of the window, swinging backwards and forwards like a pendulum.

It's Fred. His tongue is lolling out of his mouth and his eyes look as though they're about to burst out of their sockets. He's hanged himself.

I'm so completely shocked out of my skin that I can't take my eyes off him. He was only trying to help us. And now he's dead. It's the second body Jane and I have seen tonight. I glance at her. Her hands are over her mouth. I can see it on the faces of all the Lost Namers: shock and guilt, and sheer disbelief.

And now we know the extent of the demon's powers over the villagers.

"Now that's been dealt with, your turn." Ms Merrybourne sweeps her icy gaze across us. "Hmm, what to do? I could kill you right this minute. But I think I won't. Not yet. You may provide far more entertainment in the next game – watching you tear each other apart will be so much more fun!"

How can someone be so sick and actually enjoy hurting and killing kids? But then she isn't a person at all. She's a *demon* masquerading as human.

And the founders who made this terrible pact – how could they agree to forfeiting so many lives? It would have been better for the village to have suffered the same consequences of the Black Death as the rest of England.

"You'll be taken back to the school and you *will* finish the Pentangle Prize Championship games. The best must be allowed to rise to the top, and who am I to deny that? It might be one of you." Ms Merrybourne points her finger at us in turn.

"Oh and did someone ask about the previous winners?" Her eyes swivel towards Jane. "Well, if you survive round four of the games you will find out all you need to know about the previous winners." Her voice turns harsh as she says, "However, if you dare try to leave again, I *will* use my powers on you to deadly effect. Do you understand?"

Chapter 22

What's not to understand? It's pretty clear. It's either die now or die later.

I wish I'd tried to escape on that very first night after the Adder House game, after I'd watched my fellow students plunge to their deaths into the vipers' nest. Yes, I may have died trying to escape, but I would've been spared everything else I've experienced since then – all the fear, all the deaths.

And I wouldn't have Fred Simmonds' death on my conscience.

It's the middle of the night now. The Ravens didn't take me back to my dorm. I've been locked up in a room on my own.

Solitary confinement.

There'll be no more opportunities to try to escape this hellhole. It's me and four walls and a bed. The Ravens are livid because we got away from them and dropped them into a heap of trouble with Ms Merrybourne. Not as much trouble as we're in, but then they don't care about us.

We should have kept running. We should have headed out of the village and got to the next town – anywhere we could have called for help from people who aren't under the demon's influence. It's easy to say that now, in hindsight. But the clues were always there. My head sinks into my hands. That's on me. Fred told us to get away as soon as he saw us, but we didn't listen to him. What did we gain? Not much, apart from understanding how the Pentangle Prize Championship started, and why it continues.

We still don't know how to stop them, or how to kill the demon. And now it's too late.

The whole night I toss and turn in bed, trying to catch a bit of sleep before we're subjected to whatever sick game the demon has conjured up for its entertainment tomorrow. There are two categories left, verbal reasoning and spatial reasoning. And there are two houses left to host these games: Statue House and mine, Charter House. It could be either game and either house tomorrow, and it's anyone's guess what the games might involve.

Will I survive them? Will any of us Lost Namers survive them? It's been going around and around my head the whole night. By morning I'm exhausted, but still wide awake when the door is unlocked and two Ravens step inside.

One of them gives me a plate with a sad-looking cheese sandwich on it. I don't want to touch it, but I know I'll probably need the energy. I eat it quickly, gulping it down with water. As soon as I've finished it, the other Raven barks, "Move!"

I'm still fully dressed and wearing my trainers. Mum would not be happy at the state of them. They never fully dried out from the tunnels, but I'm still wearing them. They're the last of my possessions from home. I'm never taking them off.

The Ravens lead me outside. In the bright light of day it's hard to imagine the evil that lurks in this place. The tannoy clicks and my heart pounds as a disembodied voice announces the next game.

"Make your way to Statue House quad where the next game will commence shortly."

My feet don't want to take me there. My head even less so. I stand in Charter House quad, summoning up the energy to walk to Statue House. And the courage. I need so much courage. There are only twenty students left alive to play this game. I half turn, desperate to go back to the room so I don't have to face the game. But I begin walking, the sudden fear for my friends driving me forwards. Did they make it through the night? I head through the Tangle, the heart of the school. There are Ravens posted everywhere I look. Their faces concealed beneath their hoods. The sun is shining bright today, but despite its warmth on my face, I shiver. Occasionally I catch a glint of their eyes when I pass close by one of them – they are ghoulish, dead and unfeeling.

Other students join me on the walk to Statue House. I see Piers and Amy – they keep their distance from me – and I recognise a couple of the plotters from Adam's gang. We're being very closely watched. The Ravens don't want to lose sight of any of the last twenty students before the game begins – not after last night.

Statue House looms up in front of me. I follow the Raven-lined path towards the quad, trepidation building inside me with every step. What if one of the Lost Namers tried to escape during the night . . . and was taken to Ms Merrybourne for *elimination*? What if . . .

And then I'm in the quad and searching the faces gathered for my friends. They're all here! I want to hug them, but there's no chance of that as we're separated by the guards. We each place our hands, fingers splayed, on our hearts – our sign of solidarity. It gives me the courage I need.

We are herded towards the statue of Captain Merrybourne – the original Merrybourne – founder of the school, and the first sacrifice to the demon. He rises high up on a plinth, holding a scroll aloft in his right hand.

Ms Merrybourne appears from behind the statue and stands before us. She's wearing another snake-skin, form-fitting dress, crimson this time to match her red heels. Her eyes are as icy as ever.

"Who can you trust?" she begins. Her eyes sweep over us, lingering on the Lost Namers. We're the ones *she* can't trust. "You have forged alliances, which was very clever of you. Those alliances put you in good stead for the previous games. They have brought you through to this round of games, the penultimate round. This, however, will be a very different game to those that have preceded it. What will those alliances be worth now, I wonder, when you are pitted against each other one-on-one?"

The other students have grouped together in their alliances, all of them except us, the Lost Namers. But we turn to look at each other. Where before there may have been some bravado, smirking and jeering from the likes of Piers and the plotters, there is nothing but dread written large on their faces.

We're to be set against each other, which means we could be facing an ally, a friend. Anyone.

"You can run, my dear students, but you cannot escape your destiny. Today, here, you will face that destiny. Some of you will survive, the rest of you will be eliminated. It doesn't take much to do the maths for this game. Only ten of you will be left standing. Look around you. Ten of you will be eliminated."

She allows that to sink in for a moment. The hushed silence in the quad is full of dread. We're on our own.

"Game four will begin immediately. Take a look at Statue House." She gestures around her, her hands pointing towards the roof of the building. It's adorned with those nasty stone gargoyles. They're everywhere.

"It's time for you to take your place and prove that you are worthy of these walls. Are you worthy? Well, we shall soon find out. If you're lacking and fail this challenge then, like the gargoyles, you too will be turned to stone."

She beams at us as though she's bestowing a great honour upon us rather than signing our death warrants.

Failure means joining the ranks of the hideous stone monsters.

It's terrifying. I'm shaking with fear and I don't even know what the challenge is yet.

Chapter 23

Ms Merrybourne stares at our faces intently, clearly enjoying the despair she's seeing. We remain silent. No one wants to know what the game entails, and yet we need to know with a desperation that's terrifying.

Finally, the demon speaks. "The game will be a battle of wits. You will face an opponent and be given a riddle or word sequence that you must solve. The first in each pair to solve the puzzle will be deemed the winner. The loser," she gestures towards the stone gargoyles, "will become one of these delightful creatures. There will be ten new gargoyles at the end of this round. And ten winners left – the strongest, the bravest, and the cleverest of the original 100. Those ten will compete in the last game, the ultimate game."

Oh no, no, no! A word game will decide our fate? Give me a sudoku, but never a cryptic crossword. I suck at them.

What if I'm pitted against one of my friends? What then? If by some miracle I get the answer first, would I doom them to the fate I know awaits them? Could I do that to Jane or Belle or Murk or Ford? Would they do that to me?

My hands are clammy, and beads of sweat are forming on my forehead.

There's a slim chance that we won't have to face each other. There's twenty of us here. We might get lucky.

But it will be the demon who decides who we face in this game. And the demon hates the Lost Namers.

When the Ravens step back, us Lost Namers instinctively move closer together. The five of us have spent the night in solitary confinement, with too much time to think, and, like me, they have dark shadows under their eyes from lack of sleep. It's worse because we had a small taste of freedom. Then it was abruptly snatched away. All that remains is despair.

Ms Merrybourne is biding her time, revelling in making us wait, building up tension. Finally, she speaks. "Are you ready for the challenge?" she asks, sauntering casually across to us. She walks among the remaining twenty students, her eyes boring deep holes into us as she pauses briefly in front of each of us. The students she controls stand straighter and taller and smile that inane smile that shows they are in the thrall of the demon. They are ready to do anything for her.

But the Lost Namers cringe back from her. We are not under her control in the same way as the others. We never have been. How much does the demon know about why we are different? Does it have that knowledge and can it counteract it? The problem is that we don't really know why either. *The pages of the charter,* I remind myself, *that's where the answer lies.* Can they help us now?

It's too late. Ms Merrybourne is coming my way. I make myself smaller and hope like hell she doesn't stop in front of me, so I don't have to look into the demon's eyes. Her gaze alights on me, a smile twitches at the corner of her mouth, but she moves on and comes to stand in front of Jane.

Jane flinches and stumbles back a step. I steady her gently, my hand on her back. Ms Merrybourne reaches out and taps her shoulder with a long red-painted nail. Jane freezes at the touch, her eyes wide as she's drawn into the demon's eyes.

"You will face . . . hmm, let me see." She drums her fingertips on her lips before turning to Ford, who is standing on the other side of Jane. "Yes, that will be a most excellent match." She taps Ford's shoulder, before moving on.

We are stunned. The first pair has been announced and it's what we feared – two of us have been pitted against each other. Jane and Ford's eyes meet and there's turmoil within them. They know that one of them will fail this challenge and be turned to stone. There are no buts or maybes; there is only the dreaded certainty that it will happen.

Ms Merrybourne continues her stroll, sometimes stopping to consider a match, and occasionally shaking her head and moving on. It's a long drawn-out process that leaves us literally quaking in our boots.

Finally she moves away from our group, and I take a breath. Some Ravens follow her, while others are finishing off constructing the stage.

"Andy? Will you do me a favour?" Jane says quietly.

"Anything."

"If I don't make it, which is more than likely – I mean, you know how competitive Ford is, the King of Merrybourne Courts." She tries to laugh, but it sounds forced and hollow. "Tell my family, my mum, the truth about this place. Tell her everything, so she understands why I had to come here."

"I will, but I may not survive this round myself, Jane."

"You will. You have to! I want you to find my aunty.

Find out what happened to her. So you have to win!" She flings her arms around me and hugs me tight. "You won't ever forget me, will you?"

"Never, Jane." I hold her close, burying my face in her hair. I can't find the right words to reassure her. There's no guarantee that I, or any of us Lost Namers, will survive this game.

A Raven moves in and pulls us apart. He drags Jane further away from me. "Stupid bloody kids," he mutters from under his hood.

Ford is next to me now. I wonder how he'll play it. He will try to win, of course he will. We all would. *It's natural not to want to die.*

"Hey, cuz, need to say something to you." Ford has put his hand on Murk's arm.

Murk looks at him quizzically. "Go for it – we might not have much time." She nods towards the stage area where the next game will take place.

Their voices are hushed, but I can just make out their words.

". . . I know, and I wish I had more time to make amends to you. I've been a real dick – couldn't put enough space between us."

Murk's eyebrows have disappeared under her cloud of hair. "Where's this coming from, Ford?"

"Right in here." Ford points at his heart. His voices breaks as he says, "I'm sorry. That's what I wanted to tell you before it's too late. You're the tough one, the one who should be admired. You've got guts and brains and you don't care what anyone else thinks of you."

"I don't know about that," Murks says, shrugging. "It's just never bothered me what other kids think of me. I don't care if they like me or not. I've only ever wanted to be me."

"I know, and I should have respected that. Maybe I was jealous of you," Ford adds.

"Jealous of me?" Murk snorts with surprise.

"Yeah. I spend all my energy trying to be liked, trying to fit in. Even the tennis was to make the family proud. I was good at it, sure, but I wanted to be the best, to excel, for them. Not for me."

"Nothing wrong with wanting to be liked or trying to be the best at something you're really good at," Murk says. "I came here to get away and have some independence, and learn about myself, find some friends who like what I like. It was different for you."

"Yeah, I wanted to appease the fam, you know, make them proud of me and what I could achieve." Ford's mouth turns down ruefully. "But I lost myself in doing that rather than finding myself."

This is torturous. They're both talking as though this is the end, like it's confession time and they're making their peace with each other. I can't bear it. I can't bear that the demon is making us face our deaths in this way. Everyone in the whole world knows they're going to die – eventually. But to know that it will happen in the next half an hour at the hands of a friend and that there is nothing, *nothing*, that you can do about it is . . . horrific.

"Cuz," Ford says, squeezing Murk's hand, "if I don't make it, then you have to, got it? Not for me, or the family, or anyone else, but for you. Survive. Win."

"Shut up, Ford," Murk says. Her voice is hoarse with emotion. "You've got this." She puts her arms around him and hugs him tight.

If Ford's got this, then Jane doesn't. And if Jane wins, then Ford . . . gets turned to stone. I hate the demon with every fibre of my being. The anguish, the terror, the fear that it's forced on us – destroying us for its own warped sense of pleasure.

Belle moves closer to me. She's chewing her lip again; she does that when she's thinking. "Hey, Andy Chopra," she says. She smiles a smile full of sadness. "I was looking forward to this year, to getting to know the boy who'll one day be a great surgeon."

I shake my head. No. That will never happen now.

"I'm good at word games – usually," she says.

I can see the apprehension in her eyes. "Focus on whatever word game they throw at you – not on anything else," I tell her. "And hit the buzzer as fast as possible."

"That's the plan, but, you know, best laid plans and all that."

"Belle, I'm looking forward to bumping into you many more times in the future," I say, which makes her smile weakly. "I mean, outside Charter House on the first day was funny, and then in the library, that's just the beginning." I laugh. It sounds hollow even to my ears. "So you've got to smash this," I urge her.

She draws closer to me. "Likewise, Andy. You've got to win out there today too. There's still another game to play and I'll need all my friends around me." Her breath catches in her throat. We both know that we'll lose at least one of our friends in this game. Maybe more . . .

We hug like it's the last time we'll ever see each other.

A Raven moves between us, roughly separating us. "You'll get your chance to play soon," he snaps at me. He grips Belle's arm and leads her away. "You're going first. Your opponent is waiting," he tells her.

I lunge forwards to tear her away from the Raven's grip, but another Raven closes in and blocks my way.

The game is about to begin.

Chapter 24

All eyes are on Belle and her opponent as they're marched to a stage area directly in front of the statue of Captain Merrybourne, waving his scroll in the air. It seems the stone Captain wants to watch this one too. There's a podium in front of each contestant with a large buzzer sitting on the surface. So it's fastest hand to the buzzer but they'll also have to give the right answer too. It's set up like a game show – except there's no cash prize here. And you don't get to go home. My heart is pounding a thousand miles an hour.

Around me there is a faint buzz of voices as students take guesses on which one of the two contestants is most likely to win this challenge.

"Belle's good at words," Ford murmurs.

"But what about her opponent?" I ask.

We turn back to the stage. Belle is chewing her lip so ferociously she's drawn a bead of blood. She keeps glancing back at Ford and Jane, more worried about their duel than her own. It's distracting her when she needs all her wits about her to win her own duel. *Focus, Belle.* I place my hand, fingers splayed, on my chest, the rest of the Lost Namers follow suit, so she knows we're rooting for her. She sees us and gives us a small nod of appreciation. She turns back to face her opponent.

It's Adam, one of the students we saw when we were hiding

behind the couch in the old common room. He's smirking at Belle, telling her he's not afraid, but that she had better be. I don't know him, but after what Fred Simmonds said about the powers of the demon amplifying darker emotions, I wonder if this kid might actually have been OK before Ms Merrybourne bewitched him.

I can't allow myself to think that way, even if it's true. How else will I be able to play the game and doom someone to be trapped inside stone for eternity?

"Silence!" Ms Merrybourne's voice carries across the quad. "A series of word challenges, puzzles or riddles will appear. Hit the buzzer if you know the correct answer. To give you all a fair and even chance, this will be a best of three questions scenario, with the first question being nice and easy and the third a real test of your reasoning. The reward and the penalty for the winner and loser, however, remains the same. Read the instructions, hit the buzzer and shout out your answer. Nothing could be simpler!"

And nothing will kill you faster if your answer is wrong.

She claps her hands together. "Let us begin!"

An ear-splitting boom reverberates around the quad. This time there's no ticking clock, no countdown to zero. This game doesn't need them. Instead, a huge black hologram materialises in the sky above us, like an ominous thundercloud.

The first question appears.

OUT OF THE FOLLOWING FOUR WORDS, WHICH WORD DOES NOT BELONG WITH THE OTHERS?

CASPIAN MEDITERRANEAN DEAD ARCTIC

Belle's already hit the buzzer before the answer forms in my mind. It glows bright red as Belle shouts, "Arctic, because it's considered an ocean as well as a sea. The rest are seas."

"Correct." Ms Merrybourne turns to Adam. "Remember, this is best of three, so if you do not answer the next question first, then you will automatically be deemed the loser. Get it right, and a third question will be posed."

Voices rise around me. They quieten down immediately as Ms Merrybourne raises her hand and calls, "Next question."

All eyes turn to the skies again.

REARRANGE THE LETTERS TO MAKE
A WORD THAT FITS THE SENTENCE
ERBOTOTE CAN COME IN A RAINBOW OF COLOURS

The first word is an anagram. I'm trying to rearrange the letters in my head when Belle's hand slams down on the buzzer.

"Pray she has got it wrong, boy." Ms Merrybourne's voice is laden with doom when she addresses Adam. "Answer, girl."

Belle hesitates for split-second, which makes me hold my breath. Her face is in agony because she knows that by giving the right answer she will be condemning her opponent to death. "Beetroot," she says. "The answer is 'beetroot'."

Ms Merrybourne laughs. "Correct."

"No!" Adam screams, raising his hand. "Wait!"

But it's too late.

His last word is lost as his vocal chords are paralysed. Before our eyes, his arm remains raised, his limbs freezing in place, and he changes colour, slowly turning granite-grey.

Two Ravens move in and lift his rigid body off the stage and place him beside the statue of Captain Merrybourne. He's now as dead as the Captain.

Silence descends on the quad. If the consequences of losing this battle of wills was not clear to us before, they are now, for sure. The prospect of the dreadful end awaiting us is mind-blowing.

Belle stumbles off the stage and collapses on the ground. She wraps her arms around herself, and her expression runs through a mixture of emotions: relief and guilt and anger. She glares at Ms Merrybourne and I wish she wouldn't. I wish she would look away and not draw the demon's attention. Ms Merrybourne ignores her and calls the names of the next pair to play the game.

I can't bear to watch. The round ends quickly with two questions asked and answered fast. I squeeze my eyes shut when the loser is turned to stone.

And then Murk is called up.

She will face . . . who will she face? I missed the name. I swivel around to see Amy striding across the quad towards the stage. Her group are cheering her on, Piers most vocal yelling: "Get her, Amy!"

The first question flashes up in the hologram.

TWO WORDS THAT ARE OPPOSITE
TO EACH OTHER IN MEANING
SOLID RING HELIUM GAS BALLOON

Murk hits the buzzer first. "Solid and gas."

Amy scowls at Murk, and snaps, "Next one's mine!"

The next question goes up.

YOU CAN FIND IT IN SPAGHETTI,
ROAST, MUFFINS, SAUSAGES BUT NEVER
IN CHICKEN, AVOCADO, MILK OR RICE

This time Amy slams her hand down on the buzzer first. "S," she spits out with venom. "It's 'S'."

Murk looks rattled, but she quickly recovers. I can't say the same for my galloping heart rate. Murk has to get the next one right, she has to!

"We have a real battle on here," Ms Merrybourne says gleefully. "A third question will appear to decide your fate, girls. May the best of you succeed."

THE MORE THERE IS, THE LESS YOU CAN SEE.
WHAT AM I?

I know the answer. "Darkness," I say under my breath. "Hit the buzzer and say, 'darkness', Murk. Hurry!"

Both Murk and Amy's hands reach for the buzzer, but Murk reaches it a bare second before Amy and shouts the answer. There's a look of puzzlement on her face as she speaks.

Amy's face crumples. She's lost the game. I remember first meeting her in the common room in Charter House, before these games began and revealed their macabre intent, and now she will die.

"Well, there was another answer," Ms Merrybourne says,

tapping her chin, "but darkness will do equally well, and is more appropriate considering the circumstances." She turns to Amy. "As you will soon discover."

I avert my eyes as Amy screams before turning to cold, grey stone.

Murk staggers off the stage and joins Belle on the sidelines. She's shaking her head, confused, as though she doesn't understand what's happened.

"That wasn't me," Murk is insisting. "It's like I wasn't in control of myself."

My heart feels like it's about to burst out of my chest now. Is this really happening?

Belle is rubbing her back soothingly. "It's OK, Murk, you did good."

Did I will Murk to say 'darkness'? After what happened with Jane at the chapel, this can't be a coincidence. I have the Lost Namers' real names on *my* charter pages. That must be it. That must be the source of this power.

I don't want to watch anymore of these battles. I know I'll be called up soon enough, and then there's Jane and Ford's battle preying on my mind – although I could have been turned to stone before their duel.

Ford's nudging me. "You're being called."

Oh no.

Ms Merrybourne has her hands on her hips and a glare on her face. "If your name was called once more you would have forfeited to your opponent!"

I try not to look at my opponent, or meet his eye, because pretty soon one of us will be dead. I focus on the hologram in the sky, waiting for the first question to appear. My hand is tensed and ready to hit the buzzer.

WHAT IS THE ODD ONE OUT?

RAT SQUIRREL RACOON MONGOOSE HAMSTER

Easy. I hit the buzzer. "Mongoose."

"Correct. Next question."

Only now do I look at my opponent's face. It's Marco, from Charter House. I met him on the first day with Will. Will's gone, and now Marco stands before me. Playing the game is so much harder when you know the person pitted against you.

WHICH ONE LETTER STARTS ALL THESE WORDS?

-OUND -IGHT -AST -ETRE

I hit the buzzer at the same time as Marco, and we both shout out 'M', but who hit the buzzer first? I'm sure I did, but from Marco's grin he's sure he has this. If he does, there will be a third question. Ms Merrybourne pauses, letting our tension mount. Marco is hopping anxiously from one foot to another, whereas my legs have turned to jelly and I'm gripping hold of the podium for dear life.

She turns to Marco and says, "Nice try."

His face goes from smiling to desperate as it sinks in. He's changing already, his olive complexion has gone grey and his desperation is now written in stone for ever more.

I turn away before the transformation is complete, and

join the others. My chest is heaving and sweat is trickling down my back. It was close. Too close.

Piers is called up next, but I don't watch. I blank everything out. I could have let Marco win, but the need to survive is so strong that it's impossible to allow yourself to lose. There's no way Ford will let Jane win. He's ultra-competitive.

And then their names are called. Belle has turned away and Murk is close to tears. Privately, they will both be wanting Ford to come out of this alive. I'm torn by guilt, but there is no doubt in my mind – I want Jane to survive.

The first question flashes up.

WHAT WORD MEANS THE SAME AS 'PLIABLE'?
LITHE SPRINGY FLEXIBLE PUTTY

Jane slams the buzzer fast, her hair whipping around her face. "Flexible."

Murk and Belle gasp.

"Correct," Ms Merrybourne sings. She leans towards Ford, her mouth quirks in a smile. "You still have one chance – if you're very quick."

Ford's expression gives nothing away, but his hand hovers over the buzzer, ready.

"Shall we have the next puzzle?" Ms Merrybourne says.

Our eyes turn to the sky, waiting for the words to light up. My hands are clammy.

PONY IS TO CANTER AS EAGLE IS TO . . .?
EYRIE HOVER FLY SORE

Ford slams the buzzer so fast I barely see his hand move.

Ms Merrybourne turns to him and raises her eyebrow. "Oxford, I hope you have the correct answer."

"Fly," he says without hesitation.

Ms Merrybourne claps her hands. "How exciting! It's down to the last question. Sudden death," she adds in a doom-laden tone, still wearing her demonic smile.

They've both got one question right each. It comes down to the third question. The riddle. The quad is in complete silence, the tension palpable. I'm holding my breath again while Murk and Belle are holding on to each other.

Finally, after a dramatic pause, the words to the last question of these horrific games light up in the sky.

A CONTAINER WITHOUT HINGES, A KEY OR A LID,
YET GOLDEN TREASURE LIES INSIDE
WHAT AM I?

I know this. Jane might know it too – she's a fantasy geek, but she's hesitating. Ford's brow is creased in a frown as he tries to work out the answer. Then he's reaching for the buzzer.

Hit the buzzer, Jane, I scream inside my head. *Hit it!*

But she doesn't. She'll be too late. The thought of losing Jane for ever overwhelms me. I can't allow that to happen. We've had so little time together. I will her with every part of my mind to hit the buzzer and speak the answer.

Come on, Jane. Listen to me, hit the buzzer and shout my answer now! I roar it over and over in my head and her hand moves and hovers over the buzzer. *Press it and say 'egg'!*

And she does as I will her to do. A bare second before Ford, she shouts the answer I've given her.

Ford's eyes widen and his mouth falls open. He staggers back from the podium as though he's been struck a physical blow. He searches for us with his eyes. His face is a mask of despair as he's turned to stone.

Chapter 25

Jane races across the platform to Ford, tears streaming down her face. "Sorry, I'm so sorry!" she screams over and over again. A Raven drags her away from Ford's stone body to allow two other Ravens to lift Ford and place him beside the other nine stones. Ten students who were living and breathing, flesh and blood, now stand as inanimate blocks of cold, hard stone. Human gargoyles. Their faces contorted in fear and despair, mouths open in silent cries for help.

Ford's death was down to me. Inside, I'm breaking up. But there was no other choice I could have made. It had to be Jane who I saved.

Beside me, Murk is completely distraught. She's lost her cousin just as they were finding each other again. Belle is holding her, and they sob together. Ford was her boyfriend once; they shared a closeness for a time. I am the reason for their sadness. The reason why Ford was turned to stone and not Jane. It's not right. None of it is right. We wanted to find a way through it together, to be the last five.

It wasn't meant to end this way.

And me? I'm wracked through with guilt; it's burrowing through every single cell in my body. But there's relief, too, that Jane is alive. Otherwise she would be the stone statue and Ford would be standing here with Murk and Belle, and me.

What have I done?

"That is the end of this game. A very enlightening round it was too. Before me stand ten students who have proven themselves over and over again to be the best in the school," Ms Merrybourne announces.

There are four of us Lost Namers plus six. There's Piers, and Alistair's standing beside him – his new sidekick, I guess, as the rest of his posse haven't made it. Then four others whose names I picked up during the game: Harry, Emily, Ivor and Mo.

And that's it. Out of a hundred of us, only ten left. It hits like a punch to the stomach.

"You have triumphed through all manner of tests and challenges, and now you get the honour of playing the last game," Ms Merrybourne continues. "There is something else I must tell you, though." She stops until she has our undivided attention. "I recall, at the outset of the Pentangle Prize Championship, that I said there will be five winners, and each of the five will receive the prize. There is a prize – of that there is no doubt. It is the highest honour and will be the absolute pinnacle of your lives. As the elite five your names will be commemorated on the winners' plaque." She pauses. "Hmm, something has crossed my mind, though."

We freeze. What new horror is she about to throw at us? What could be worse than has already been done to us?

"I may have said five winners . . . well, I lied." Her cackle rises as she takes in our stunned faces.

What?

She lied?

Of course she lied.

So there won't be five winners? Will there be ten? Was that the last game? A flame of hope flickers briefly, but the demon douses it with her next words.

"There will be one. One ultimate winner. One to take the most coveted prize."

There is a collective intake of breath as Ms Merrybourne's words sink in. We will die here in this hellhole. There is no escape. I don't believe there is an ultimate prize at the end of it either. There never was. This was simply to provide the demon with entertainment – much more thrilling than simply killing us as this year's sacrifices. No wonder the villagers can't look us in the face. They're alive because of us.

"And as for the final game," Ms Merrybourne continues. "It promises to be the most exhilarating of all. I cannot wait! All ten of you must fight each other to the death, until one victor emerges."

Fight to the death? Like gladiators? Except we're not gladiators.

We're students. Not killers.

"Until then, my dears." Ms Merrybourne disappears with a chilling smile.

We huddle together – me, Belle, Murk and Jane, as we face the other six remaining students. Piers has somehow made it through the rounds virtually unscathed, but he doesn't seem as full of himself. We've all lost friends. Piers has lost all but one of his posse, and how loyal will Alistair be now that it's sudden death? But Piers is tough, with a rugby player's build, and if Ms Merrybourne really means us to physically fight to the death, then Piers will likely be the last one standing.

I draw the Lost Namers away. It's pointless having a face-off with the others. That time will come soon enough when the next game starts. I need to tell them about my charter pages and what I think is happening. But if I tell them the whole story and reveal the level of control I have over them they might not trust me any more. They'll turn on me, maybe on each other, and the last thing we need is to be fractured. We need to stick together in case there's a chance that we can topple the demon.

There has to be a way, and I really think my power might be the key. I have to risk it and tell them. It might save their lives, and hopefully they'll trust me if I come clean now, before the final game. They'll see that I'm not keeping it secret or as a silent advantage. If I leave it any longer then they definitely won't trust me.

"There's something I need to tell you," I begin.

They cluster around me as I tell them what happened in the tower when the Raven was chasing Jane and me up the steps. "He'd got hold of Jane's foot and was dragging her down. I – I sort of willed Jane to kick him with her other foot, and I envisioned the guard falling down the stairs and banging his head, so we could get away."

They're staring at me, confused.

"So?" Murk says. "That's what any of us would have been thinking with our lives at stake. And if I were Jane, I would have done the same thing, instinctively."

I'm thinking about how to clarify things when Jane speaks up. "It wasn't instinctive for me," she says, eyeing me strangely. "I . . . I didn't feel like I was in control of my body."

"Hang on. What do you mean by *'willed'* and *'envisioned'*, Andy?" Belle asks.

"I don't know, but I . . . I think I *made* it happen." I stumble over the words, barely able to look my friends in the eye.

"What? How could you possibly make it happen?" Murk's voice rises.

"The pages that I ripped out of the charter book and kept. They've got your names on them. Your real names." My palms are clammy and my mouth feels dry. "I think it allows me to control you in some way."

"You've got to be kidding me!" Murk looks bewildered, but then I see the moment something clicks. "I knew something was off in that game! I felt like – like someone else was in control of my mind and made me act. You pulled the same trick on me as you did Jane."

"Murk . . ." I reach for her in a panic, trying to explain, but she shrugs me off.

"There was a weird moment when I had an out-of-body experience. It was brief, but it happened," she says. "I thought it was the stress, the unbearable tension of getting the right answer and slamming that blasted buzzer as fast as possible. But that was you! You gave me the answer: darkness. I was going to say 'fog'."

"I don't know. I knew the answer and said it under my breath. You know the way you will your friends to get the answer right, especially with so much at stake. That's how it was. It wasn't planned or anything. It might not even have been me," I finish lamely.

Murk clenches her fists. "It *was* you!"

"And you're alive." I look at her pleadingly. "Please, Murk. It wasn't intentional. I had no idea it worked in that way."

Jane is staring at me intensely. She's put two and two together and worked out how she won. I'm pretty sure she knew the answer was egg, but she didn't hit the buzzer fast enough. So I willed her to hit it, and that's how Ford lost. Belle's caught the look on Jane's face. Without saying a word, she steps back uncertainly. She knows too.

I am a pariah. They don't trust me.

It's Murk who dares to ask. "Did you *will* Jane to hit the buzzer and speak before Ford?"

Fear and shame are coursing through me. I don't know how to tell her I caused the death of her cousin. So I don't answer her.

"Did you? Did you choose Jane? Answer me, Andy!"

I cover my face with my hands. When I look up at her, I whisper, "Please forgive me. I didn't even know I was doing it. One of them was going to die."

"It wasn't up to you to make that choice!" Murk yells.

"Andy . . . how can we ever trust you again?" Tears are falling down Belle's face. I can't bear the way her eyes are full of disappointment.

"You can. I promise you. Please."

"Then destroy the pages," Murk demands.

"I – I can't do that. We need this power. Listen, please," I beg them, but they're already turning away from me. "Give me a chance to explain." I run around in front of them. "Please!" They hesitate.

"The charter pages are the key. I didn't ask for them,

and I had no idea of the power they contained when I took them. Ask Jane. I did it because I'd messed up the first page, and everyone would know it was me with my crossed-out name at the top," I say quickly. They're listening. "I can use the pages to help us – all of us. And if I have to use that power again it will only be to save you."

"Like you saved Ford, huh?" Murk snaps. She draws away from me. "You have a power. Like the demon. And you used it against one of *us*. One of your friends. No way can we be anywhere near you." She takes another step back.

I try to lock eyes with Jane. At least she should understand – I saved her not once but twice. But there's no forgiveness in her eyes as she looks away from me.

I see something else in her eyes. It's in all their eyes.

Fear.

"Wait," I plead.

They turn their backs and walk away from me, the three of them. My last and only friends in this hellhole. Our friendship is in tatters. The Lost Name Society is no more.

My whole world crashes in on me. I want to chase after my friends, call them back, explain things better, but my knees buckle and I collapse to the ground. They've made up their minds. They want nothing to do with me. I've terrified them with my power, with what I can do with it.

What have I done?

I'm on my own.

Chapter 26

The Ravens close in on me. One of them yanks me off the ground and half-drags me across the quad.

"He'll be the first to go next," he tells the Raven walking beside him. "He's got no stomach for what's to come."

"Yeah, if he thinks that little word game was terrifying, wait until the real battle begins."

They laugh at me, sneer at my weakness. They're not wrong. I always said I wasn't a fighter. How did I survive this long?

Because of my friends.

The next game is a fight to the death. If I don't escape before it begins, I'll die here. We all will – Jane, Belle and Murk. I need to get us help.

The Ravens march me back to Charter House, to the room they locked me in last night. It's upstairs, on the second floor, well away from the dorms and the common room downstairs – not that the only other Charter House student left, Piers, would help me even if he could hear me calling. There's no one to help me now.

I weigh up my options. There's no way I can overpower two Ravens. They're taller and stronger than me. I can't use my power to make them help me, but maybe I could try to appeal to them.

It's not easy talking to someone when you can't see their face, and they're always concealed beneath their hoods. I try my luck anyway.

"Please will you help me? I just want to talk to my parents one last time. I won't try anything, I promise. Please."

"Are you hearing this?" one Raven says.

"Thinks he can make requests now," the other one sniggers. "He'll be asking for a three-course meal next."

The Raven tightens his grip on my arm, clamping it hard between his big, meaty hands. He brings his face close to mine. All I can see is the dark shadow beneath his hood. "You don't get any privileges here. You'll get something to eat later. That's about it."

"If we remember," the other says.

They laugh as they leave the room. I hear the key turn in the lock. It was worth a shot. I slump onto the bed, rubbing my arm where the Raven had it in his vice-like grip. The locked door taunts me. There's no forcing my way through that heavy oak door without a key.

Above the bed there's one arched window with a wide stone casement. I push off the bed and try the handle, even though I know it's locked from trying it last night. I press my head against the glass.

My window faces the back of the school, and there are Ravens patrolling the grounds. With only ten of us left and four of us locked in solitary confinement, I don't know why they're bothering. I guess they have their orders, and after our failed escape attempt, they're more vigilant than ever. Not even they want to incur the wrath of the demon.

I lie back down on the bed, and curl up on my side, my knees drawn to my chest and my head buried in my hands. Getting out of here would be nothing short of a miracle, but I need that tiny bit of hope to get me through the long hours until nightfall.

The last thing I want to dwell on is what waits for me at the end of those long hours. A battle to the death.

Those pages from the charter are still in my pocket. It feels like they're burning a hole, but I don't touch them. They're what have got me into this trouble in the first place. No. It wasn't the pages. It was me, the way I used them. Maybe I can use them again – to get the Lost Namers to forgive me for Ford's death. The inescapable truth is that one of them was going to die anyway. And how can Jane blame me for wanting to help keep her alive?

It wasn't my choice to make though, was it? And if I force or try to influence the others to forgive me then what kind of forgiveness is that? It wouldn't be real. I can't even forgive myself for any of it. I have to find a way to win them back and make things as right as they can be before the game tonight.

And that's an impossible task.

I should never have come to this school. All I ever wanted to do was make my parents happy and work hard to become a surgeon. That might make me sound like a nerd, but who doesn't want the best for their future self? I know I do. Mum and Dad, they believed in me, pushed me, always so certain that I would go further than they had ever had the chance to. I was going to get into the best school, the best university, and become a renowned surgeon.

Their dream was my dream. The teachers at my old school used to put me down or overlook me, and never thought I would amount to much. If I messed about, I would get into more trouble than the white kids. If my work wasn't up to scratch, I would get marked down more. I sucked it up because my parents said I had to. "Always keep your eyes on the bigger picture," they'd say. I even went along with it the very first time the teachers started calling me Andy. It was embarrassing, it made me angry, but I kept my mouth shut.

"'Andy' is so much easier to say than 'Aniruddha'," Mr Pendred had said. "So we'll put your name down as 'Andy' in the register, OK?"

The whole class had heard him and I squirmed in my chair as they laughed along with the teacher. And that was that. Aniruddha became Andy.

I did everything 'right'. As much as any kid can. Lucky for me, or unlucky for me given the present circumstances, I always knew what I wanted. So if the teachers couldn't be bothered to say my name properly and wanted to call me Andy, then fine. It made my life easier going through school. I had my family and I had my mates.

A fierce pain stabs through my heart. I miss them so much. I wish I could use the charter pages to take me home – but they're not like a magic carpet or Aladdin's lamp. They don't come from a good place. They come from evil.

I need to think about good things. I've got so many happy memories, I should spend the rest of my remaining hours alive remembering them. Some of the best times with my mates were the FIFA sessions at their houses or mine.

We spent hours playing football in the park without a care. One time, when I was goalie, I broke my finger. I twiddle the middle finger on my right hand. It's never been the same again. A war wound – the good kind. Not like the ones I've got from this place.

My parents were never that strict and let me play for hours, but they always had high expectations of me, which somehow got transferred to me through some strange kind of osmosis. They were much more concerned that I ate proper food. My mum's aloo tikkis were the best – delicious, fried potato patties oozing with spices and sprinkled with fresh coriander. My dad's special chicken biriyani made properly with a pastry crust I always broke through first, releasing its warm fragrant steam before plunging my spoon in.

My stomach grumbles. OK, I shouldn't think about food, or my parents' faces. Otherwise I will end up crying. I'm suddenly utterly homesick for my life with them. Even when my mum used to tell me off. I can hear her voice now. "Aniruddha Chopra! What were you thinking?"

I sit up. What *am* I thinking? I *should* be thinking about them and my life before. I need something to help me want to survive this ordeal.

What are the others thinking, alone in their rooms – Murk and Jane and Belle? We're separated, left only with our own turmoil for company. I hope they're all right. We could use each other's support now more than ever. It's our friendship that has kept us alive.

I pull out the charter pages and look at the Lost Namers' signatures.

Names matter. The charter proves it. But I stuff the pages back into my pocket. I can't use them in the same way I did before.

I will make my last stand and I will do it in a way that I'm not ashamed of. I will win my friends back, and I will do it right.

Chapter 27

Beyond the treetops of the Merrybourne woodland, I watch the sun set, lighting up the sky like a fireball of oranges and reds, before dipping its head, fading, and finally dying to darkness.

Earlier in the evening, the Ravens had brought me another sad-looking cheese sandwich. I ate half of it. The other half sits on the table, its edges curling in disgust. I'm going to have to eat it soon. The Ravens refused to tell me when the last game will begin, but I can't enter whatever arena they have planned for the battle to the death with an empty stomach –that's one thing Ford taught me. I play some Central Cee tunes on my phone while I eat it. We both like him – liked, I mean, because Ford is dead. We might have had a lot more in common if we'd been given the opportunity to get to know one another.

I grimace as I chew the dry bread and plastic cheese and vow never to eat another cheese sandwich for as long as I live. Which may not be long, as I hear the key turning in the lock. I almost laugh at the timing. I swallow the last mouthful.

I'm ready.

They lead me out to Charter House quad. Ravens surround it, their huge torches aflame and flickering against the backdrop of the house, casting an eerie glow. I'm the only contestant here, which makes me freak out for a minute. I clench my hands by my sides, and feel the familiar trickle of sweat running down my back.

One by one, the others arrive: Murk, Belle, Jane, Piers, Alistair, Emily, Mo, Ivor and Harry. They are led into the centre of the quad, eyes wide with terror. I try to make eye contact with Murk, Jane and Belle as they take their place in the quad, to let them know that they can trust me. Hard to do without words. I raise my hand, and place my splayed hand on my chest in our salute. It hurts like hell when the Lost Namers turn their eyes away from me.

I've got to somehow focus on the game and save my friends, whatever the consequences. How's the game going to work? I glance around the quad and take in the circle of pillars surrounding it. There's a Raven standing beside each column. Something has been placed on the flat surface at the top of each pillar, but I can't make out what. I squint harder. That pillar closest to me seems to have a . . . is it? *No, no, no.* It can't be. It's horrific – a metal stick topped with a spiked ball. Murk would know its name. Do they seriously expect us to use a weapon like that on our fellow students, on our friends?

I glance up at the top of the other pillars. More weapons, but I can't make out what they are. I don't even want to know.

Ms Merrybourne glides into the centre of the quad, her hair flowing around her in the breeze as though it's alive, her face whiter than white, and her lips painted blood red. In her hands she holds the charter.

"Here you are, the final ten, the crème de la crème, the best of the best," she begins. "You have now had the opportunity to take in the details of my beautiful arena. Did you notice what wondrous things lie atop the stone pillars? I do hope so, because you may find them necessary to be victorious. There are a variety of weapons you may choose from. Of course, you will not be able to simply climb to the top of the pillar to get to your weapon. That would be an impossible task." She laughs. As though we haven't already been asked to complete impossible tasks. "This is where you will need to use your spatial reasoning. Ravens!" she calls out.

A group of Ravens begin to roll in different sized blocks and place them haphazardly in the centre of the arena.

"You must build your way to the top of the pillars," she says, delighting in our bewildered expressions.

What? How? I look more closely. The blocks are all different sizes and shapes. Anyone great at spatial reasoning will work out how to fit them together fastest – and reach the prize at the top. The weapon.

"You will have to be quick," she continues. "Whoever gets their weapon first will have a head start on the others and may begin their attack immediately."

My heart plunges into my stomach and I feel utterly sick when I see what the pillar next to me has placed on top of it.

An axe.

I cannot ever, ever, ever imagine wielding it on anyone – even my most hated enemy. From the horrified expressions of the other students, I know I'm not the only one with that thought.

Ms Merrybourne opens the charter. "I would like to

remind you that you have all willingly signed your names in the charter. You may not have known it at the time, but let me tell you what that means. You have signed away your right to freedom for *eternity*. Each and every one of you will fall under my control – as and when I need you. It will be an existence of eternal servitude."

We all look bewildered. So does that mean we don't properly die? We serve the demon for ever?

I'm still trying to absorb her words and their meaning when, from the edges of the quad, students begin to file in.

Lots of them.

Their pace is steady, their heads are held high, but it's their faces that get to me. They're blank, utterly devoid of expression. As they approach, I begin to recognise many of the faces. I see Will and stagger back from him. He's alive! How? But there's nothing in his eyes, no emotion, no recognition, nothing. He stares right through me even as I shout his name.

We're surrounded by all the students who fell in the earlier rounds.

The ones we thought were dead!

I search for Ford, but he isn't among them. It's the students who fell in the first three rounds. Small solace, but at least by being turned to stone, Ford was spared an eternity of serving the demon. The fallen students encircle us.

They are alive, living and breathing, but like empty shells, soulless and servile. A terrible negative energy radiates off them, but Ms Merrybourne raises her arms in rapture, fuelled by it.

"Do you see how vital you are to me? You sustain me. You give me power, my dear students."

So this is what the tree roots do – they suck out our energy and pass it to the demon. And so long as these games are always played every twenty-five years, the demon will never, ever, die.

"Five students win each championship – on paper," Ms Merrybourne continues. "However, there is only one student who is deemed worthy of the ultimate prize. And what is that ultimate prize, you might ask? It's *me*!" she roars.

What is she talking about?

"Only one soul, as in preceding years, is worthy of me. Every quarter century I must merge with a new soul, and it's with the soul that possesses the most potential for greatness. The winner of the Pentangle Prize has the chance to join me and become more powerful than they can even imagine. Power is the essence of existence."

I'm reeling from what she's telling us.

Essentially the demon is reborn and made more powerful every twenty-five years. Fred Simmonds told us that Captain Merrybourne was the first to do this. And Jane's aunty . . .?

What did that mean for her as the winner of the 2000 games?

"Another little twist for you. Of the Merrybourne students who've played my games, all go on to graduate from the school. All go on to achieve notable things and gain important, significant positions. And all of them remain under my control. My influence stretches far and wide, well beyond these walls – beyond Merrybourne itself."

That's how she does it! It's not that deaths are covered up. No one dies, they're just stripped of their souls. They belong to the demon.

The truth is too much for us to comprehend. We gape at each other, the final ten. Are any of us willing to join the demon to get what we want?

Am *I* willing to merge my soul with the demon's?

No. No. No. No!

The flames of the torches flicker and go out for a second as a sudden gust of wind squalls around the quad. It's followed by a stream of hot air, which soars around and around the arena. The torch flames once more burn bright.

"I see wonder on your faces," Ms Merrybourne says.

All *I* see is terror.

"And let me assure you," Ms Merrybourne continues, "it *is* the most wondrous honour that only the winner will truly appreciate."

Then, she asks playfully, "Is the victor ready to emerge?"

Chapter 28

Judging by the expressions of the remaining students in the game, their answer is a resounding no. Merging with a demon? Is she crazy? Does she really think that any of us would willingly want that?

But it's a matter of life and death. Or is it? Whether we live or die doesn't matter as in either case we have no free will. If we die, we are then reborn to live a life controlled by the demon – like the soulless, spectating students who fell in the previous games. Will. Marco. Alex. And so many others. Or, one of us becomes the sole survivor, the chosen one, and is absorbed by the demon.

What a choice! We're doomed either way.

Jane breaks away from the Raven guarding her. What is she doing? The demon will have her killed on the spot.

The Raven goes to grab her, but Ms Merrybourne raises a hand. "Let her approach."

"I want to know what happened to my aunty," Jane declares.

"Your aunty?" Ms Merrybourne looks surprised.

"Seung-min Park. She was a winner of the last Pentangle Prize. Where is she?"

"Ah. I know exactly who she is," Ms Merrybourne answers with a devilish grin. "She was indeed the winner of those games. A great competitor. Strong and intelligent, and she made the best choice for herself, for her future."

"My aunty wasn't like that. She was good and she was kind and she cared about people!" Jane yells. "What have you done with her?"

"Let me show you," Ms Merrybourne replies, the smile never leaving her lips.

Very slowly, Ms Merrybourne's face begins to undergo a transformation. Her features blur and shift. They form a freaky squashed-up plasticine face, with holes for eyes and a wide yawning space where the mouth should be. They change again, a small nose appearing, the mouth shrinking, lips forming. Ms Merrybourne's snake-like hair withers away, but before she becomes totally bald, short dark hairs sprout from her scalp. It's horrific, but we can't tear our eyes away. We watch, rapt as Ms Merrybourne mutates into another person entirely.

And then the change is complete.

Ms Merrybourne now wears the face of another woman. Her silky dark hair is cut in a short bob. Her eyes are small and set deep, her lips a thin line. The woman looks a lot like Jane. The family resemblance is undoubtable.

"Ji-yeon, I know you don't know me, but I'm your aunty, Seung-min. It's good to finally meet you, my dearest."

Jane's mouth opens and closes, her face a picture of horror. "No. No!" She's shaking her head. "This isn't happening. You can't be her. How can you be her? It's not possible." Jane's voice is trembling with emotion.

"I am, dearest niece. You came here for me and that makes me so proud. I had the same determination, the same strength of will as you've shown. And look where it's led me! I defeated everyone in my championship and won the ultimate Pentangle Prize." She flings her arms out. "The power I wield is beyond imagination. I can do anything, anything at all."

Tears are rolling down Jane's face. She never would have believed that her aunty would accept the demon's offer. Not even after Ms Merrybourne told us that the winner of each Pentangle Prize gave their soul to the demon and merged with it. Even then it was too far-fetched for her to believe – for any of us to believe. But the evidence is right in front of us now. We cannot deny it. Every single word Ms Merrybourne spoke is true.

"This can't be happening! Mum spent years and years searching for you. I came here to find out what happened to you. And all that time you were here? You cared nothing for the people you left behind. You destroyed our family. Your sister, my mum, remember her? She's never recovered from losing you. How could you do that to us? To the people you loved and who loved you."

"I had to make a choice," Seung-min says. "I chose this path. I urge you to take over after me. Be victorious. You have it in you to be truly great, Ji-yeon. Your power will know no bounds. And you'll live for eternity."

Jane screams. She rushes towards her aunty, but a Raven seizes her and drags her back. Seung-min smiles at her niece one last time and then her face begins to crumple as she morphs back to her previous form.

Once again, Ms Merrybourne stands before us. She's enjoying our disbelief, revelling in our horror.

And now that everyone knows that Jane's aunty merged

with the demon when she won the last games, they're looking at her in a strange way, and I have a horrible feeling in my gut. They'll attempt to eliminate Jane first, before coming for me and Murk and Belle, just in case the demon is biased towards Jane in any way.

As for the Lost Namers – they believe that I control them. That I'm like the demon. I can't bear the thought.

I step forwards.

"Jane, Belle, Murk." They turn their heads towards me. I take my charter pages out of my pocket. I could have used these to help us, but they won't help me or the others if there's no trust between us. I need their trust back, and this is the only thing that might restore their belief in me. I can only hope. It's all I have left.

I scrunch up the charter pages and toss them aside. It's more than a symbolic gesture. I'm telling them that I'm their friend, a Lost Namer like them, that I will stand with them against the other competitors, against the demon.

"I didn't choose my nickname like you all did. It was given to me by my form teacher, Mr Pendred. 'We'll call you Andy', he said, without asking me if that was OK, or if I minded. I've lived with that name for a long time. But it's not my name. Aniruddha is my real name and I am reclaiming it. It means unstoppable, invincible, courageous. I'm going to live up to that now." I face the demon. "I will not fight my peers. I refuse to take part in your sick games. I will fight you, demon, for my life and theirs."

Ms Merrybourne simply raises her arched eyebrows and smiles and nods at my little speech, before bursting into peals of laughter. When the laughter dies, she says, "Fine words, and worthy of a winner. But you will still have to earn that place, and that can only be earnt by killing your peers."

"I refuse to kill them. There's only one being here who must be stopped at all costs, and that's you!"

Ms Merrybourne frowns at me, unable to understand why or how I am capable of defying her. Her eyes flick to the charter pages lying discarded on the ground, and realisation hits her as to the real reason why her influence hasn't worked on us. Her eyes narrow. Her hair writhes around her head like a hotbed of angry vipers. "What have you done?" she howls, her voice laden with fury. "What have you done?!" she repeats, spittle flying, face contorted with rage.

It's epic seeing her perplexed and angry. Those charter pages were the key, but in the end they were useless to me. I need my friends more. I sense a shift among the remaining competitors too, and it feels as though there may be hope for us. It makes me more confident, stronger. Perhaps all is not lost.

Up in the sky, a countdown clock has appeared. It's counting the seconds down before the last game begins.

The battle to the death.

0:10

0:09

Jane steps forwards. "My real name is Ji-yeon Park and I will fight for the honour of my family. I will not give myself to you, demon. And if I die, I will die fighting with my own name."

0:08

0:07

Murk and Belle step forwards and make eye contact with me and Jane. The palms of our hands slap our chests in our five-fingered salute. It's a declaration that the alliance is back. The Lost Namers are back! And we will fight together.

0:06

0:05

Ms Merrybourne has regained her composure. "Your stupidity seems to know no bounds. There are six other finalists who are anxious to join me. And they will kill you and each other to do it. You four will simply die by their hands, and if not by theirs, then mine."

0:04

0:03

The Lost Namers take in the stance of the other six competitors. Each and every one of them has murder in their eyes. They're out for themselves and they're out to win. It's clear they've resolved to join the demon.

0:02

0:01

The loud boom signifying the start of the games thunders around the quad. The Ravens and our fellow fallen students fade into the background. Will's dead eyes stare through me and I know that I will not, cannot, end up like that, an empty shell at the beck and call of a demon. I harden my resolve.

Let the games begin.

Chapter 29

My hands are shaking, and I'm already drenched in sweat even though the game has barely begun.

We come together, the Lost Namers, and get in a huddle.

"We need a plan, fast!" Murk says.

"Not dying is the main plan." I grimace. "We have to kill the demon – somehow."

Jane balks, but quickly recovers. "Yes, it has to die, but one of the other contestants might get to us first."

She's right – Piers has venom in his eyes and it's directed at me. Luckily he's only got Alistair on his side. "Murk, you're our secret weapon. How's your spatial reasoning?"

"Yeah, pretty good. I'll get us a weapon from up there." She's already checking out the blocks, how to position them so she can get to the top of the pillar.

"And the rest of us?" Belle asks.

"The rest of us will go for the demon," I tell them.

"Sooner the better!" There's steel in Belle's usually soft brown eyes.

"Follow me."

The arena has erupted into frenzied motion. Murk is scowling, a look of fierce concentration on her face, and she's muttering under her breath. I really hope she's got this. She takes another second to assess the pattern and then springs into action, throwing blocks together to make steps to the top of the pillar.

Three contestants are charging towards Murk, targeting her, going for the same weapon at the top of the pillar. It's Harry, Mo, and Ivor. We double back to help her. Murk faces off against Harry, her body a blur of motion. I tackle Mo, while Belle and Jane are avoiding punches thrown at them by Ivor as they try to bring him down. There's shouting and screaming and I know one of those voices is mine. I lash out with my fists, adrenaline rushing through my veins. Mo lands a punch on my jaw, which has got to hurt him more than me, but the pain judders through me. I kick out, but Mo's rushed off for another pillar. Harry is crawling away from Murk, and Ivor now thinks better of facing the four of us and darts off.

There's no time to stop, no time to take stock of what's going on, or where Piers might be. Has he managed to reach a weapon already? That's the moment I'm dreading.

"Go!" Murk yells at us.

She's on her way up, climbing up and then down again for another block, building her structure higher and higher. I can't watch her any longer. I have to focus on the demon.

Ms Merrybourne is at the centre of the arena. Her face is in raptures at the utter mayhem around her.

I don't stop to think. Rage takes over as I launch myself at her, knowing this is the last thing she's expecting. Her eyes widen with surprise, but I don't let her recover. I barrel into her with all my strength, surprising her again, and myself, with the sudden surge of power within me. The charter slips from her fingers as she tries to defend herself. She raises her hands and attempts to push me away, but I've got a good hold of her. We're struggling – me trying to hold on with everything I have and the demon trying to hurl me off.

My eyes flick to the ground where the charter is lying open, unattended. It's the key. If the charter did not exist, then there would be no demon, no more Pentangle Prize Championship. Nothing. I suddenly know what has to be done.

The charter must be destroyed.

But how? The names have to be crossed out, or – or . . . I've got it!

"Grab the charter, Jane!" I yell. "Chuck it in the well. Hurry!"

The well water will wash away the names on the pages. It will free the other finalists from the demon's control. It will free everyone who signed it, including the walking dead.

It was something I never thought of before. But then the charter was always behind glass, protected by a spell, or a curse.

Jane races towards the charter and snatches it up from the ground. She darts off towards Well House, dodging a couple of Ravens who try to stop her, ducking and diving between the blocks and the pillars around the quad. She's fast and makes it out of the quad, disappearing into the darkness of the school grounds as some Ravens peel away and make chase. I pray that she makes it OK.

The demon is enraged and her strength is a terrible thing. I don't think I can hold her for much longer. Belle joins the fray and throws herself at the demon. But with a terrible shriek, the demon twists and hurls Belle to the ground.

My hands slip and the demon sneers at me before throwing me off too. I land beside Belle, breathless and bruised.

Belle clutches her side, gasping for breath.

"Are you OK?" I ask her.

"Could be better," she groans. "How are you able to match the demon's strength?"

"I don't know," I respond. I look at my hands. Where did that sudden burst of power come from?

Ms Merrybourne screeches, "Arise!"

From the shadows, several figures emerge. Belle and I look at each other, our eyes wide as we realise the demon is calling forth the fallen students from the previous rounds. "Go," she orders them. "Stop the girl."

Oh no! She's sending *them* after Jane too.

The fallen students turn, and, as one, they break into a horrifying run through the quad, not caring about us final ten or the blocks in their way, just running at the demon's behest as her hands move in the air, directing them out of the quad towards Well House. We have to stop this demon!

"Andy!"

It's Murk, and she's got a sword. I love that girl – her timing is impeccable. She slings it off the top of the pillar to the ground, and I'm suddenly faced with the fact that the only sword I've ever held is a little plastic one in primary school.

No time for self-doubt! I scramble for it while the demon is distracted. Someone barrels into me, shoving me out of the way.

Piers. He grins at me as he aims a kick, his nostrils flaring. He puts everything into it. I sidestep and grab hold of his leg.

He totters on one leg for a moment, a look of bewilderment on his face, and then I push with all my might. He lands heavily.

I waste no time and pick up the sword. At first it feels heavy, and I've no idea how I'm going to be able to wield it. There's no time to wait for Murk, the skilled martial artist, to get down from the top of the pillar. There are mere seconds while we have the element of surprise: while the demon is controlling the fallen student puppets. I heft the sword in my hands and it begins to feel lighter, I swish it through the air, making an arc, before I turn towards the demon. I take a breath. This is it. I allow the anger, the rage, the fury to build up inside me.

And attack.

With a burst of speed, I lunge at her, my sword raised high, putting everything I have into it. She sidesteps my attack easily, laughing. I lunge again, and again she twists away, avoiding the blade of the sword with ease. Again and again, I attempt to thrust the sword through her, but each time, she's faster.

What did I expect? She's a demon. But I won't stop. I have to give it everything.

"You're boring me now," she scoffs, as I make a desperate lunge. My momentum carries me forwards, taking me too close to her. She sees her chance and lashes out with a fist. I see it coming towards my head. I duck away, but not quick enough, and the punch connects like a brick to my head.

It sends me spinning off balance. Black dots leap and dance before my eyes. I hit the ground with a thump, the sword coming free from my grip and landing too far from me.

"No!" I grit my teeth through the pain, reaching desperately for the sword. "Belle!" I cry, but Emily has got hold of her and they're locked in a struggle, grappling on the ground. There's no way she can help me. I need the sword.

My body is screaming in pain, I roll across the ground, my fingertips almost touching it, almost . . .

Ms Merrybourne's foot stamps down hard on my hand. The pain brings tears to my eyes. My plan is failing. Kill demon: I failed. Or be killed – which is just about to come true.

As I clutch my hand to my chest, cradling it, Ms Merrybourne stoops down and retrieves the sword. "Forged centuries ago by the most skilled craftsman, it is the finest weapon of them all – in the right hands, of course. In the wrong hands," she smirks, "it's less than useless."

I try desperately to get to my feet but she kicks me back, and comes to stand over me. The sounds and cries of combat in the arena fade into the background. I have eyes only for the gleaming point of the sword that is pointed directly at my chest.

This is it. This is the end. No one can say I didn't try my best.

I imagine the point of the sword turning away from me, turning instead towards the demon's body, the way it should have been if I had been stronger, faster, more capable. The sword is not my weapon. I should have left it to Murk, but there was no time. What can I do now? Hope for a miracle? Simply *will* the demon to turn the weapon on herself?

I do both: hope and will.

The tip of the sword judders. It shakes. Then it begins to move away from my chest. It rises upwards, and inch by slow inch, it turns itself around in the demon's hands. Ms Merrybourne's eyes widen, her mouth caught in a rictus of disbelief. Her face contorts with agony as she fights to turn the weapon away from herself.

"How are you doing this?" she growls. "Tell me!"

The sword falters slightly as I lose focus.

The demon throws back her head, the snake-like tendrils of her hair dancing around her, and laughs manically. "Andy Chopra, did you think you could best me? Do you think a mere sword could destroy me?"

The sword begins to move away from the demon. I clamp my eyes shut, close off my ears to the demon's words, so I can't see her or hear her mocking me, laughing at me. I need to focus, to dig deep to find the strength that I need to will the sword to finish the demon. I will it with everything I've got.

The demon shrieks. I open my eyes to see the sword acting upon my will.

I scrabble away as fast as I can. I don't understand how, but I'm able to make the demon turn the sword on herself.

It comes back to the charter again, I'm sure of it. I'm able to control my friends because their names are on the charter pages I'd ripped out during the first assembly. But I don't know the demon's name.

Hang on. I remember now that I wrote the names of every single one of all the previous winners – right from when the games first began centuries ago – on the back of my charter pages. That's the name of every soul that the demon has ever taken and absorbed into itself. They are part of the demon, and the source of her power.

Which means . . .

I must have control over the demon too, or, at the least, I can fight her on level terms.

I will the demon to point the sword at her chest and then to fall on it. I will it with every fibre of my being. With a look of sheer horror and incomprehension, the demon begins to do exactly that. The point of the sword reaches her body. I will her to plunge it into her and fall forwards.

The lethal blade of the sword plunges into her heart. A blood-curdling cry erupts from her, and she begins to fall, the sheer horror of what is happening reflected in her wild eyes. Her face turns towards me as she topples and falls to the ground. Her eyes are open but the sword is buried deep in her chest right up to the hilt.

Ms Merrybourne's face begins to mutate as the demon assumes the form of every single past winner, all the souls the demon has devoured. They appear and disappear in rapid succession – brown eyes, blue eyes, deep-set eyes, they bulge and contort with the rest of the face; lips and noses shrinking and expanding with terrible, ghastly expressions. It's a horrific sight to behold, but I cannot tear my eyes away. As the demon's form flickers and morphs, the screaming begins. I clamp my hands to my ears, but to no avail – the sound pierces deep into my head. It's the sound of the voices of multiple people merging in a bone-chilling chorus. Their voices rise up in a crescendo of dread that splits the air around us, echoing and reverberating, and causing the ground to shake and rumble beneath me.

Without warning, the voices stop. The ground stills and silence descends on the quad. The demon writhes one final time in her death throes, and then she shatters in an explosion of such fierce light that it burns through my eyes.

Chapter 30

Around me, Piers and the other finalists are emerging from the demon's trance, rubbing their eyes and gazing in confusion at the quad.

Then I glance towards the fallen students, wondering what'll happen to them. Will they crumple into a heap and die now that the demon is gone?

But no – it's as though they're awakening, confused and disorientated, staring at each other in wonder. But alive!

The Ravens are already backing up, suddenly feeling threatened. Their hands are outstretched, as though that will keep the students at bay. They're making for the shadows, hoping to get away before the students fully emerge from the demon's control. Too late. Chaos breaks out in the quad, the students' voices rising into a clamour as they rush around in bewilderment. They want answers and only the Ravens can give them those. I watch as they stoop to retrieve discarded weapons. And turn on the guards.

They advance menacingly on the Ravens, who are shouting back, defending themselves. Some of them get away. Others aren't fast enough and they're outnumbered. It won't be long before the students have overwhelmed the guards.

Belle and Murk rush to help me up. Their sheer relief is tangible as they throw themselves into a hug. I'm dazed, still in shock – I can't believe that it's actually real. Somehow, against all the odds stacked against us, we've defeated the demon. She's gone. For ever.

"We did it!" Murk cries.

I glance around the quad, searching desperately for Jane. My stomach is in knots again. "Not yet," I say, shaking my head. "Jane hasn't come back."

"She's got to be OK, hasn't she? The demon's dead," Murk says.

That mental image of the Ravens and the controlled students racing out of the quad to chase her down on the demon's orders comes back to me. But what might have happened in those minutes before the demon exploded is uppermost in my mind. "We've got to find her!" I say, panic rising like bile in my stomach.

As we race through the grounds of Merrybourne School, we encounter more fallen students. They look lost and puzzled. By the time we reach Well House quad, my heart is thumping hard with fear for Jane. I should have taken the charter to Well House myself. I put Jane in danger. If anything's happened to her it will be my fault – and I couldn't live with that.

The light is dim in the quad. I'm looking around so frantically I almost miss her. And then I spot her. She's slumped on the ground, her back against the well. Her arm is flung over her head as though to protect herself. She's not moving.

"Jane! Jane!" I shout.

Her arm drops away from her head, and she opens her eyes as we call her name again. She's alive, and the relief is overwhelming. A ghost of a smile creeps onto her face. She stumbles to her feet as we join her.

"You did it!" I pick her up and swing her around. "You destroyed the charter!" I set her down. "Are you OK?"

"Yeah, just about. I didn't know what to do. They were after me, but I managed to throw the charter into the well before they got hold of me. There were so many of them, trying to grab me." Jane shudders. "And then they suddenly stopped. They let go of me and backed off. It was weird, like they were waking up, or something. I don't know. I couldn't work out what was going on." She's talking fast, the words flooding out of her.

"It's OK. Everything's OK now," I tell her.

"What do you mean?"

"The demon's dead. Andy defeated her," Murk says, clapping me on the back so hard I almost stumble forwards.

Jane's mouth falls open. "What? How?"

Their eyes turn to me. They're expecting an answer. I don't want to tell them that I *willed* the demon to turn the sword against herself. I can't, so I deflect the question. "I don't know if she's really dead. She could have just gone back to wherever she came from. Anything's possible."

"Well, she exploded like a mega firework, that's for sure. There's no trace of her left, and everyone who was under her control is now free," Belle says. "And the charter is destroyed. It has no hold over anyone any more."

"She's gone?" Jane asks.

There's a faraway look in her eyes. She must realise that by killing the demon I killed her aunty too. I don't think she's completely processed that, or even thought about how she'll ever be able to tell her mum the real truth.

"I don't know," Murk replies, running her hands through her cloud of hair. "I don't feel safe. We need to get away from here, away from the school and the village, as far away as possible. Then we might be."

There are only a few dazed students left in Well House quad; most of them have fled. I don't see any Ravens, but they could be lurking anywhere. "I agree. I don't want to spend a minute longer here than I have to." I drop my voice to a whisper. "The guards won't want witnesses to what's been going on here, will they?"

"Right, we need a safe way out then," Belle declares.

"Wait! I need to go to Statue House first." We turn to Murk. "There's a chance that Ford might still be alive. The other students are, so why not Ford? I need to find out."

She's right. A flicker of hope lights up in me. There is a chance. I made sure Ford lost the game and was turned to stone and that guilt weighs heavy on me. But what happened in that penultimate game was different to the other games. It was the only game where students were turned to stone rather than being fed to the roots of the oak. All the way to Statue House I'm hoping against hope that the curse has been reversed and that Ford is free of the stone he's imprisoned within.

"Look!" Murk points towards the statue of Captain Merrybourne.

He's no longer surrounded by ten other stone gargoyles that were once the students. Instead, we see some students wandering aimlessly around the quad. I count them – there's nine.

"He must be here too!" Belle cries.

We search the quad, and finally spot him. He's standing there, no longer a grey hunk of stone, but as still as a statue, hands hanging loose by his side.

Murk rushes to him and throws her arms around him. "Hey, cuz! You're back!" she cries. I can hear the sheer happiness in her voice.

"Good to have you back, Ford," Belle says, hugging him.

Jane and I hug him too.

His eyes search our faces, as though trying to remember who we are. He opens his mouth to speak, but shuts it again. He shakes his head, his eyebrows furrowed together.

"Take your time, Ford." I tell him.

"Ford?" Belle squeezes his hand. "It's me, Belle."

He looks blankly at her.

Now I'm worried. "Do you know who we are?" I ask him.

Finally, he speaks. "Um, yeah. But what's – what's happened?"

"It's OK, cuz, take your time," Murk reassures him. "You were a block of stone a few minutes ago!"

"What? How?" he says, bewildered.

"It's OK, Ford," I say. "What's the last thing you remember?"

"The last thing? Um, I was – I was pressing the buzzer. Too late. And then – and then nothing. Nothing." He pats himself down. "I lost the game. How come I'm not a slab of stone?"

Murk relates what happened in the arena, in the final game – the battle to the death – and as she does, Ford's eyes widen. "You serious? You guys have done all that? Sorry I couldn't help out, but I was a bit stuck, haha!"

There's a collective groan from us, but we're all grinning, relieved.

Ford is back.

"Way to go, LNS," he says, punching the air and hugging us all. "Proud of you guys. Truly."

My utter relief for us all being reunited ebbs away when the image of Ms Merrybourne and her Ravens storming into Fred Simmonds' house comes flashing back. Our euphoria at believing we had escaped was dashed in that moment of terror. How wrong we were.

"We need to get out of here, guys," I say. "I'll feel a whole lot safer when I'm at least a hundred miles from this hellhole!"

"So, which way?" Belle asks.

"The front gates?" Murk suggests.

"Hmm, not sure about that. They're probably locked and barred," I say. "The guards won't want us escaping and revealing all the murky secrets they've kept concealed for years."

"The same goes for Merrybourne village," Murk adds. "They've got too much to lose."

"Agreed." Belle is chewing her lip. "Fred's brother, Jim Simmonds, is the mayor of the village. He's played a huge role in supporting the demon and the games. He allowed his brother to be killed to keep this secret. For sure, he'll be sending out search parties to find us once he's got wind of what's happened."

"What about the underground tunnels?" Jane says. "I've still got the map on my phone, although the battery's almost dead. I can remember most of it though."

"Enough to find a route out of Merrybourne School and the village?" I ask.

Jane nods. "Pretty sure. The network of tunnels is extensive. The game was only played in a small section of them. It seems to go on for miles."

"Then that settles it. But there's something we have to do first," says Murk. Her mouth sets in a determined line. "Come on, help me."

She storms over to the statue of Captain Merrybourne. "Time he hit the deck!" She climbs up onto the plinth and begins to push. She's struggling on her own, but other students in the quad join her. We clamber up and join the effort. He weighs a ton, but, inch by inch, Captain Merrybourne begins to shift. We set our shoulders against him and heave, groaning and grunting with the effort. We manage to get him near to the edge of the plinth. I cast around for something to help us move him. There's fencing along one side of the quad. I jump off the plinth and wrestle a plank of wood free.

"Everyone push here while I slide this under him," I instruct the others. "Now!" They heave and I slide the wood under the statute. "OK, one last shove should do it! Heave!" I cry and then he's toppling and falling, all the way down to the stone flags below, splintering and shattering into hundreds of pieces.

Above us, the shadow of Merrybourne School looms high. Still standing. We can't tear it down with our bare hands, but we won't rest until the village is exposed and this place comes crashing down. We can't let this happen to anyone else ever again.

A board I hadn't noticed before catches my attention. I step closer to see what it says.

"What is it, Andy?" Jane asks, peering over my shoulder.

"It's the names of the past winners." I grab a splinter of stone and add my name.

The rest of the LNS follow suit. It's good to see our proper names on the board.

Aniruddha Chopra

Ji-yeon Park

Mercedes Campell

Trixibelle Clayton

Oxford Ike

That's us. The Lost Name Society.

We're alive. We survived.

And I make a silent promise to myself that Merrybourne, with all its twisted secrets, will not.

THE END

IF YOU LIKED THIS YOU'LL LIKE:

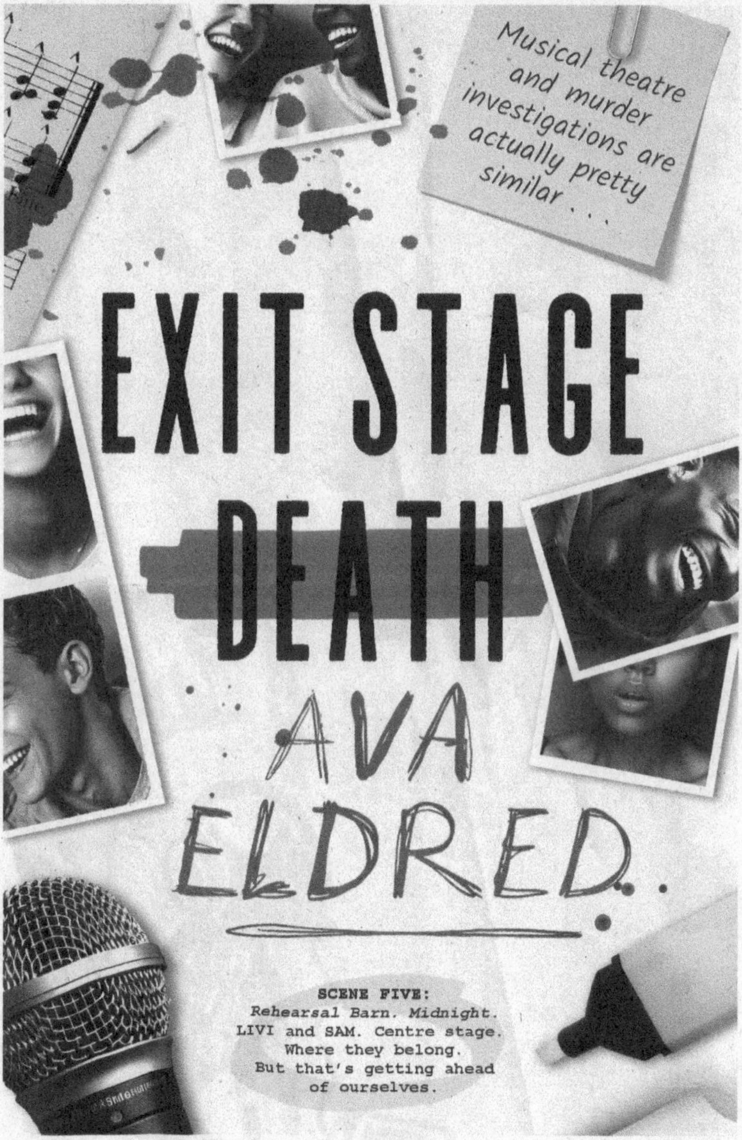
Musical theatre and murder investigations are actually pretty similar . . .
EXIT STAGE DEATH
AVA ELDRED
SCENE FIVE:
Rehearsal Barn. Midnight.
LIVI and SAM. Centre stage.
Where they belong.
But that's getting ahead of ourselves.

HAVE YOU EVER WONDERED HOW BOOKS ARE MADE?

Fox & Ink Books is an award-winning independent publisher specialising in Children's and Young Adult books. Based at the University of Lancashire, this Preston-based publisher teaches MA Publishing students how to become industry professionals using the content and resources from its business; students are included at every stage of the publishing process and credited for the work that they contribute.

The business doesn't just help publishing students though. Fox & Ink Books has supported the employability and real-life work skills for the University's Illustration, Acting, Translation, Animation, Photography, Film & TV students and many more. This is the beauty of books and stories; they fuel many other creative industries! The MA Publishing students are able to get involved from day one with the business and they acquire a behind-the-scenes experience of what it is like to work for a such a reputable independent.

The MA course was awarded a Times Higher Award (2018) for Innovation in the Arts, and the business, Fox & Ink Books, was awarded Best Newcomer at the Independent Publishing Guild (2019) for the ethos of teaching publishing using a commercial publishing house. As the business continues to grow, so too does the student experience upon entering this dynamic master's course.